FR

David Harsent was born in 1942. He has published
four books of poetry, all with Oxford University
Press: *A Violent Country* (1969), *After Dark* (1973),
Dreams of the Dead (1977) and *Mister Punch* (1984).
He lives in London.

DAVID HARSENT

From an Inland Sea

A King Penguin
Published by Penguin Books

Penguin Books Ltd, Harmondsworth, Middlesex, England
Viking Penguin Inc., 40 West 23rd Street, New York, New York 10010, U.S.A.
Penguin Books Australia Ltd, Ringwood, Victoria, Australia
Penguin Books Canada Limited, 2801 John Street, Markham, Ontario, Canada L3R 1B4
Penguin Books (N.Z.) Ltd, 182–190 Wairau Road, Auckland 10, New Zealand

First published by Viking 1985
Published in Penguin Books 1986

Made and printed in Great Britain by
Hazell Watson & Viney Limited,
Member of the BPCC Group,
Aylesbury, Bucks
Typeset in Palatino

To Jane

Acknowledgements

Parts of this novel have appeared, in slightly different forms, in *Granta* and *Firebird 3* (Penguin).

THE SECOND YEAR

*

May

After a while she extended her hand, palm-up, her elbow a pivot on the side of the cane-bound chair. His own hand didn't move. Undeceived, he knew that she was putting the sun to the white skin on the underside. There was a seam in the sea where a deep blue met the harbour's aquamarine. He sat with her outside the St Patrick's Hotel, coffee untouched, watching the bright boats rise and slide on the swell. He lodged his forearms on his own chair so that the shadow-pattern of their fingers interlaced. She was unaware of that tiny violation; even so, she moved her position and sighed.

'Do you want to move on for lunch?'

She didn't reply, so he said her name. She jerked like someone coming awake and swerved in the chair, her arm circling in a fluent motion to collect her coffee cup. Raising it to her lips she sipped and asked what he'd said. 'I was dozing,' she explained.

'Shall we move on somewhere for lunch?'

'You like it here, don't you?'

'I do. I thought perhaps . . .'

'Yes, why not. Pay the bill, then.'

She got up and walked very slowly to the low wall where the sea stopped. She was thinking of something. There was almost no noise: the foam lipping the sand, a fan ticking when he went into the hotel to settle up. No birdsong, no undertone of insects. Each day she loafed through the midday scorch; he survived it at her side, shining with cream under the panama, looking for cafés where he could order a coffee to have the water that came with it. He had made plans, constructed tactics, to stop the harm he was doing. He'd thought about giving up drink. Perhaps there were ways of enlisting her help, or offering some sort of hint. He suspected that she had her own plans. Nothing was

3

predictable except her manner of devising silences while his apologies were absorbed.

When he emerged she was sitting on the wall, chin on raised knees, her arms crossed on her bare shinbones. The video in his head clicked and the tape started to roll. She lay under the man, her thighs sharply angled and clasped in either hand to keep them hoisted. Her mouth opened in the two or three seconds that brought her to the edge until she shouted into his face, wide-eyed with pleasure. The man slowed his stroke, letting the sensation spread and settle. He dropped his head and browsed on her breast, kissing the nipple cleanly. After a time he gazed at her steadfastly until she looked directly up at him. They both smiled. He began to work into her again. She gave a small croak of approval and folded her legs on his back. It was all logged: the interior, the time of year, the name. He didn't even try to guess what these involuntary agonies were costing him. On each occasion he felt as if he were biting pieces out of his own face.

She watched him step out of the umbra of the doorway into the light and walk over counting his change with an expression of gloomy hostility. It made her smile. She cared for him enough to want to make him happy, but he seemed to lack the talent for that. It required too simple a vocabulary. Sometimes, particularly when she had wilfully hurt him, she had to consciously remind herself of her feelings: like counting blessings. Loving him was an outmoded thing, contradictory and oddly virtuous; it was a sort of patriotism.

You could tell from the photographs they took just how hot it was: a piercing white statue of the saint on its plinth near the harbour wall; the stone shone; she knelt to set it against a backdrop of noonday sky while he wound down the car windows.

A mile or so from the next village he saw the Christ atop a scrub-cluttered hill. He judged it to be at least fifty feet tall. The arms were outstretched in blessing or supplication. She pulled

4

over and he got out with the camera, standing on the bonnet to line up the shot. She wagged the front of her blouse to make a draught and watched his knees flexing.

'It'll be a dot.'

'Will it?' He bent and peered at her through the windscreen seeking more advice.

'From this distance. Just a smudge.'

'I suppose so.' He tried a few more angles, but didn't press the shutter-release.

Much later, after their lunch and the wine they had agreed, that morning, to forgo, he came to on the rock they'd scouted for – secluded so that she could take off her bikini top – and said: 'I could have climbed up to it and taken a picture.'

'Why didn't you?' Her breasts and the strap lines were salmon pink, the rest a deep brown. She trailed her hand across her belly where the perspiration itched, then eased the crotch of her briefs with a forefinger. 'I'd have driven on and found a table.'

'Well, it would have been a bit of a walk.'

'Don't be wet.'

'I didn't think of it,' he said.

She sat up to get the bottle of suntan cream and shaded her eyes. 'You've burned.' She had been using his shirt and shorts as a pillow. Now she tossed them over, looking concerned. 'You'd better cover up.'

His skin crawled as he put the clothes on and shuffled into the triangle of shade near her head. She held out the bottle. 'Do my back while you're there.' To make it easy she sat up and turned away, dangling her legs over the water. A windsurfer rounded the outcrop of rock and, when he saw them, man-oeuvred to a halt, stepping round the *planche* to change direction. Holding his balance, the man looked at her, lowering his sail a little to lose the wind, then beyond her for a moment to where he crouched applying the cream. The board drifted in until it was no more than twenty feet away; the man's eyes were fixed on her; his feet trod the *planche* to keep it stable. She held her

5

hair up while he smoothed cream across her shoulders until it clarified, then patted her to let her know it was done. Swinging her legs round she knelt to rearrange her towel and finally subsided, sighing, her shining back presented to the sun.

'Another fifteen minutes – okay?'

'Yes, fine.' He rummaged in their tote bag for a book. When he looked up, marking his place with a finger, the windsurfer was heading away, raising a wake as he took the breeze further out.

Going back, she slowed the car, but didn't stop, when they reached the stretch of road that gave the best view of the hill. 'Too late now.'

'Yes.' The wind was cool. He shivered as he leaned out of the window for a clear look. The outlines were odd. The robe was a solid T; the long oval above it he read as a fall of hair; but then it seemed rods protruded from the full sleeves: thin and rigid and without hands. It might have been modern, or vandalized, or crudely done.

'It's extraordinary.' As if in response she brought the car to a near halt. He wondered if he might be making too much of the thing: might seem precious. He said: 'It is curious, isn't it?'

She nodded. 'They're a very seriously religious people, I gather.'

He felt chilled, his skin burning and prickling, so he wound the window up. 'Southern Catholicism,' he said. 'Irresistible.'

'Oh?' She speeded up. 'I thought you inclined to the hard men of the north. Lindisfarne, hair-shirts, winnowings to the bone – all that.'

'Yes. There's something about the southern version. It's indulgent, corrupt. I don't know . . . it attracts me when I see it.'

'Or childish.'

'Oh, yes; that too. In theory, I find it contemptible.' He was thinking of the blaze of neon haloes they'd seen in Venice; the charred remains of a martyr looking like ossified roots, a foot in its glass box. Relics, all over the city, packaged like putrefying orchids. 'How far, would you say, does superstition stand from faith?'

She glanced sideways, noticing the lack of draught from his window, then back at the road as she fumbled for the sidelights. 'Oh dear,' she said, 'I'm afraid you're going to suffer.'

When he took his clothes off she hissed through her teeth and laughed sympathetically. 'Oh dear.' Apart from the shallow vee that had been protected by his trunks he was uniformly scarlet.

'Shit,' he said softly. In the mirror, dimly lit, he was almost luminous. His skin twitched. There were strong, intermittent pains and it burned. He felt as if he were standing too close to an immense electric fire. His teeth chattered.

He lay for half an hour in a brimming bath of cold water while she stayed on her bed, reading. To break her silence he called out for a brandy. 'Do you think you should?' she asked.

'It's that or sex. Or both.' He climbed out of the bath and took the glass she offered. 'Any distraction . . .'

She handed him a towel. 'How about dinner? Any good?' She had changed into black silk trousers and a white shirt that showed off her tan.

They dined at the fish place, their favourite, under vines and lapped by bougainvillea, and he shook so that his knees kept rapping the underside of the table. Then they drove back to the hotel and she took him to the bar for his eighth or ninth brandy. A formica-topped circle had been laid down for dancing. They sat at the bar and watched the same three couples quickstep to everything the band played, then – at his insistence – went out and bopped to a ragged rendition of 'Don't It Make My Brown Eyes Blue?'. He was feverish and had to bite his lower lip to keep his mouth still.

In the room he took another brandy from the mini-bar, then undressed in a rush, yelling. She looked at him, standing at the foot of her bed, arms held away from his sides, his cock up and ticking with pressure. 'You're mad,' she said, lying back and parting her legs, using a finger to make herself ready. He bent over so that she could wet him, briefly, then covered her. She jacked her thighs away from his burning flanks. He moved slowly, allowing her nothing. She looked up at him, interestedly. When he started to come she asked, 'Doesn't it hurt?', intrigued as if she were watching someone being tattooed. He slumped, without resting on her. Her heels slid down the counterpane. He thought that the only way he would get through it would be by talking all night, sitting out on the balcony, maybe, drinking water, registering the moment-by-moment relief as his skin cooled towards morning, waiting for the sky to dim and lose its darkness, then grow increasingly pale until it gained the tinge of a lighter blue and the sun lit what it could touch from the horizon, but her eyes had already begun to flutter and the tiny wheeze beneath each indrawn breath lengthened as her limbs relaxed.

THE SECOND YEAR

*

July

Today was nice. I drove to Richmond Park and walked down to the lake. Small parties of people strolled this way and that through the bracken and between the trees. They looked preoccupied by purpose. The scene resembled the prelude to a story which would, in some way, involve these groups: a serial drama to which each would bring some particular quality. I could imagine a movie camera picking up on that elderly couple taking slow steps along the gravel path by the water; on the young marrieds with the blonde infant in its pushchair; on the iron-grey lady in green tweeds accompanied by her son – she talked earnestly, walking a pace ahead as they strode towards the fringe of a wood; on the family picnicking on a slope between two herds of deer; on the man and his dog descending to the lake on one stretch of a familiar circuit. Perhaps we would hear fragments of conversation that would, at first, mystify us, though later grow startlingly clear as the narrative took a new twist and the role of one group or another became established. The mother and son intrigued me most: their animation, the small distance that was preserved between them. She would cast a glance at him now and then to emphasize some remark. He walked with his hands weighing down his jacket pockets, his head lowered, nodding from time to time. You could sense the fingers making fists. The line of his jacket was drawn to them. She turned her back to him without concern, a narrow, green, upright, punchable back. The best he might manage, you'd think, would be to make a face behind it as she crossed the *sol y sombra* line into the trees. In fact, as if her broaching of new terrain were a real separation – something permitting an unexpected choice – he hesitated before following her in. How long would it be before her monologue broke to await a response,

11

before she looked back, before some evaporation of tension told her that her signals were no longer striking the target and returning? He checked without altering his pose, standing with head down and arms straight as pistons, his pockets bulging. It was for no more than five seconds that he hesitated before following: starting off with a long stride to catch her up. It was odd to feel such curiosity.

The mother and son drew me along a path I don't usually take. It seemed their very purpose was to inveigle. They were out of sight by the time I reached the point at which he had taken after her. It was odd; made me feel . . . not better – energetic.

The dog went to and fro after squirrels until I leashed her so that I could fall into my thoughts. I'd been playing Haydn's *Theresienmesse* and it had occurred to me that music's ability to reach us so directly is its greatest drawback: that universality, that common touch. I shuddered for what I shared. This letter's fabrications will, of course, let you know that it was never written to be sent; but already I suspect I mean 'should not be sent' and that it will incur your impatience on Wednesday morning as you sip tea in the – what do they call it? – refectory? The theory that Haydn provoked was a cosy, spiteful thing and I refined it carelessly in terms of some other human events: desire, religious conversion, childbirth, falling in and out of love. All in all it was a pretty unrewarding chain of thought. The randomness of things makes all response a kind of selfishness: not an original notion, and I was sorry to have reminded myself of it.

You can imagine where it led; and I remembered, in particular, the days we spent in Scotland when all our weaknesses were held in abeyance and the deceits we practised on other people were part of an adventure that became a collection of anecdotes as it was happening, each episode seamlessly joined to the next and establishing itself as a memory at once. We would sit in the bar of some remote hotel, or drive to the next selection from the map, reminiscing about the day before. And I was as delighted with your role in the turn of events as you were with mine. I don't think we missed a thing; we were word-perfect.

Other people's recollections – what are they? What brings them to mind? Some outlandish occurrence: a just-past-dawn drive on a road between high banks, strewn along a five-mile stretch with the crushed corpses of rabbits? A fable of contentment: the log fire illuminating a panelled room, sounds outside of a storm-wind and the sea, rain turning in spirals under the porch light? An accusation: making love among roadside trees, or while the maids sat outside patiently smoking and chatting; or in the car, at dusk, too agitated by the lust that derives from closeness, release, a deserted landscape and speculation to wait for the next hotel? All memory is mythical, we are already agreed on that.

But how strange it is to have starred in one's own history. I thought of the house I grew up in, peopled by women, and the image came back to me of one of them laying a table for Sunday lunch. The faces are interchangeable: each must have performed the task hundreds of times before some meal or other, though the method never varied. It seemed to be autumn; a fire was burning fiercely; we would have returned from church maybe fifteen minutes before and someone had swept the hearth and added fresh logs. Now it was drawing strongly behind the wire guard and I'd moved to sit beside it, not directly in front where the heat was too great. The room had been cleaned and tidied. There was a freshness about the brisk flow of yellow flames into the chimney-neck.

I sat on the carpet, reading. They bought me a book every week and gave it to me after church. It was too early in the day to think of the weekend as almost gone. The gloominess of late afternoon was very far away. We hadn't had lunch; the room was warm but not yet heavy; there was bright, cold light from the tall windows; the book was only just begun.

One of them entered the room and took a tablecloth from a sideboard drawer. I watched as it was allowed to fall out of its concertina-d folds along the centre of our dark, oval table. Then she lifted her arms suddenly, an extravagant, joyous gesture, and the heavy white cloth opened with a crackle, full-bellied like a spinnaker, hiding her from view before it slowly settled. She brushed it with her palm, then slid it to and fro, adjusting to make the overhang even.

I went to wash my hands as I always did at the moment when knives and forks were being put out; and went from bathroom to kitchen, as I always did. The other three were there, each performing the set of tasks she always performed, sharing a joke about that morning's sermon. They were gently capable. In all things they enjoyed a doctor's licence to have nothing hidden from them and I accepted that. It was a benign and wise community. They were there when I took a shit – they taught me to wipe myself. They would aim my little acorn of a cock before I was properly awake. Their hands moved over me to scrub and brush, to button and knot. They squared off the days. They conspired to know things. Knowledge possessed by one would immediately, it seemed, be possessed by all without the need for instruction. Finding something to smile at, one would smile, then each in turn as the insight spread. The smile appeared to pass from mouth to mouth. Over lunch, their laughter was perfectly judged to make me laugh. I didn't know what the laughter was for, except that it made a round of mirth that I could help to construct, bringing end to end at one point of the oval table. I traced the drawn-out, pleasant, indulgent rhythms of gossip.

I remembered, too, how formidable they seemed, how completely self-possessed when it came to a picnic or an outing to the zoo. Their quiet words with one another affirmed that *this was so*, that *this should happen next*. Those journeys, however, seem to have been rare. I recall the fire and the book, the just-cleaned, uncluttered room, the billow of the cloth, the arms flung up. I recall the domestic to-ings and fro-ings that went on round me. I was part of an enclosed order. If the cloth had settled over me as I lay on the floor, had I felt its draught on my face as it belled with the woman's flourish, then seen it descend to

envelop me – not a white tablecloth, but a black pall – I might
have known, somehow, what it meant and have welcomed it. I
might have been glad, becoming one who was dead to the
world. If love came in to all that, then I'm pleased that it should
have. What I remember, I think, is devotion and the unques-
tioned mysteries that the women provoked. Mother, grand-
mother, great-grandmother, aunt. There are two lines from a
hymn often sung on those Sunday mornings: *When, before my
Father's throne/I shall know as I am known*. It was more comfortable
to be known. I rarely felt any real need to be part of our lives'
practicalities. Naturally, I didn't rationalize it in that way, any
more than I worried that some intrusion, someone else's
presence, might render the women's way with me banal. It was
not until much later that it became apparent how the world
could be organized according to other predilections.

What images of you do I choose? It might be too soon to tell.
It might always be too soon. I used to like you best in moments
of passion, the selfish garnering of sensation that stretched your
features before leaving everything blank for an instant, but that
was before I could think of how commonplace such incidents
were in your life. It's pleasant to watch you when you suspect
that I'm watching. I saw you, once, in a church in Italy, pay for
a candle and kneel before one of the saints, expecting to be
observed – was it Francis? – even though you had sent me to a
nearby shop for food. Your goings to bed, your hurryings
through the mirror business each morning . . .

I developed a taste for strong feelings. One of them would
read to me, one in particular, supported by four big pillows in
the bed she went to at eight o'clock each evening. Her room
smelled of lavender and sometimes faintly of brandy. On
occasions she'd ignore my choice; but, as often as not, she
would take the book from my hand, nodding in a serious
fashion, and turn to the place I'd have marked with a strip of
paper. There existed a number of fine possibilities: the best,
perhaps, Noyes's *The Highwayman*. Each time she began I would
feel a pang of pleasure. I had duped her into doing something

from which I gained a physical response that, then, I couldn't define but which, now, I'd probably describe as seedy. To a lesser degree, it was something I could do for myself, but the experience was never so strong as when I was passive.

> Back, he spurred like a madman, shouting a curse to the sky,
> With the white road smoking behind him and his rapier bran-
> dished high.
> Blood red were his spurs in the golden noon; wine-red was his
> velvet coat;
> When they shot him down on the highway,
>   Down like a dog on the highway,
> And he lay in his blood on the highway, with a bunch of lace at
> his throat.

When that passage was reached, I'd look away as my face flushed and balance my tears on the brink, almost letting go, then holding back: maintaining a poise that constantly promised release while never quite permitting that wastefulness. The skin on my neck, on my thighs and upper arms, would crawl deliciously in spillage after tiny spillage of heat. At times, it would affect me so that I'd feel as if I'd been struck in the back by the heel of someone's hand – jerking forward, the breath catching in my throat. I thought it a wickedness, but couldn't have said why. Something to do with drawing such intensity off; something to do with the woman's unawareness, as she read, of what I was getting from what she so blamelessly did.

I became a glutton for the sensation, but didn't, so far as I remember, deceive them in anything else. I believed we were indivisible. Occasionally, they would mark their difference by mentioning matters that lay not beyond my understanding, but beyond my recollection. I didn't mind. Such tokens made them old, and underlined the authenticity of their guardianship, and made me lucky. I was conscious of still possessing all my life.

There was another time – when you were sidling down the slope towards our valley. You had wanted to go on your own, but the day was promising so I had reasoned that you wouldn't object if I found you and walked back with you for the last half-mile or so. You were where I'd expected you to be. I stood still to watch you descending. What surrounded you seemed vast: the whole valley-side of cropped turf, an unmarked sky. You came crabwise, purposefully, barely heeding the place, or so it appeared, and I tried to tell what portion of herself a person alone in such space might retain. I wanted to know what could be shed, what weight of behaviour. But when you looked up you simply waved as someone will who steps from a train and sees, at the far end of the platform, the one who had said he would be there.

The iron-grey lady and her son, together with the couple and their blonde baby, arrived in the car park just as I was about to drive away, so I watched them. The camera wouldn't have liked the young family. They were sullen and looked to be making a duty of their outing. The child was loaded into a small chair strapped to the back seat of their car; the pushchair was folded and put into the boot. It was done with morose efficiency, as if the lives of all three were governed by dull tasks of that sort. I imagined that the husband would be a good driver and would own a metal tool-box containing many compartments.

Iron-grey and her son had resolved their differences: they were walking together. The boy pointed something out and his mother looked along the line of his arm, then smiled and nodded. It must, I thought, have been she who had compromised or admitted fault and now she was taking pleasure in the virtue. They were both handsome – signs of delicate good breeding in their long faces. The director sent them for tea in the nearby tea-shop – an impromptu scene – asking them to make it look as though this was only possible because their quarrel had ended. Iron-grey, the more experienced, naturally, injected a clever bit of business by taking the boy's arm as they approached the gate leading to the tea-shop's garden. It left the impression that she was beginning a slow, covert advance from concession to control, moving back over lost ground. An admirable touch.

Well, I drove home, cooked a meal, fed the dog and mopped her paw-prints off the kitchen floor. I remembered to draw back the curtains, but it was almost dusk. I bled the radiators and gave the plants some water. Before you left you made yourself a cup of tea and drank half of it. I have preserved it: it stands on the kitchen table where you left it. The tea has developed a creamy film on the surface, seamed by tiny fissures. I expect the arrival of your taxi prevented you from finishing it and stopped you, too, at page five of that morning's paper. I can see only three items on the page that might have drawn your eye and have read them a number of times, hanging over the folded sheet without disturbing it. If I bother to eat at the table, I use the other end. Your end has the paper, the cup, and an ashtray containing only ash – so you must have kept your cigarette in your mouth while you carried your case and opened the front door. I can see you squinting against the smoke, the dangling cigarette looking mildly incongruous between your freshly painted lips, and especially because you were wearing that elegant suit with the slim, calf-length skirt and the waisted jacket, your cameo brooch on the lapel to complement your pearls.

I have opened your wardrobe and when I read in bed I can glance up, when I care to, at your clothes, which seem to have about them a forlorn, abandoned look. They are inert: the not-chosen. I wonder why you took the rings you took, not those still on the spread fingers of the ring-stand. Among other things, this little museum contains the objects you are saving for another time. The ashtray, paper and cup, of course, are different. There's a vibrancy about them. They possess something of the dramatically arrested activity of the *Mary Celeste*.

None of this is as obsessive as it sounds. It is done for my amusement: a kind of experiment in reconstruction. Clothes, cold tea, jewellery, the jumble of letters and bills in your desk drawers, the sachets of herbs among your underclothes, scarves and neatly folded blouses. Each day all stays as you left it and each day I try my response: do I find differences in the objects, do they reveal something new, is it possible to interpret them in some different way? Whose terrain is this?

I don't go out much. I'm growing a beard which will probably come off before you get back. I found, in one of your diaries, my name and my old address – my full name. The inscription struck me as stark and lacking expectancy.

He signed the letter and sealed it, leaving it propped up against a vase on the dining-table as they always did. On Saturday he received a picture postcard letting him know that she was well, reminding him of a task she was sure he'd have forgotten and reaffirming, succinctly, that she loved him.

THE SECOND YEAR

*

September

'Shall we go to the taverna today? Do you want to?'

He turned and looked at her as she levered herself up on one elbow and shaded her eyes with her free hand. Tiny patches of sand, stuck there by sweat, blotched her breasts and flanks. There were crumbs of sand in the strip of pubic hair and a dusting of it in the damson-coloured crease where her buttocks began.

'I don't mind.' He tried to anticipate her. 'We've got the bottle of water. I'm not really hungry.'

'It's such a hike all across that vineyard.' She watched the others who had come on the boat getting ready to leave the beach, the girls pulling on T-shirts and bikini bottoms, the men getting into shorts. Manos was rounding them up and herding them towards the inland path, his cigarette-holder jutting from the side of his mouth and twitching up and down as he spoke round it to give instructions. 'We mus' be here once more by three o'clock,' he said. 'The sea is perhaps not soft then.'

'It's just a fiddle.' She rested her chin on the backs of her hands and watched them waiting in a group before being led off. 'That repulsive man has some sort of deal with the taverna owner; we don't have to eat; we've paid for the boat.'

Manos came over to where they lay, stamping through the sand, clapping his hands. 'You are coming for food.' She turned her head to the side and closed her eyes.

'I don't think so.' He looked up at the gigantic paunch swathed in blonde fur, the half-hidden trunks tight over the bundle of genitals; then he sat up to confront the man more directly. 'No. Not today.'

Manos looked sulky. 'Good food. Fish come from here,' he gestured out to sea, 'today. Salad. Feta cheese. You like it all.'

23

'I think we'll just hang on here, okay?'

'Okay.' He turned round and waved the others off. 'At three o'clock we leave. All mus' be on this beach.'

'At three? That's earlier than usual.'

'Today a wind will come. It is difficult for boating.'

'Repulsive,' she said after he'd set off across the beach. 'He must be every day of forty-five . . . that ludicrous teddy-boy haircut.'

They usually travelled to the beach with a different captain on a smaller boat. That morning, though, it had been Manos's turn to take the trip. He'd lowered a bucket on a rope from the jetty and made the passengers wash their feet before going aboard: that was the first indignity. Then, when they'd reached the near-deserted beach, he had anchored in deep water, worried about going aground. She had jumped off and swum round to the prow, then lowered her feet. 'I can just touch bottom here,' she'd yelled. 'If you jump over me – beyond me – you'll be in your depth.'

'Are you sure?' He'd stood on the very edge, holding on to a rope. 'What if there's a hollow or something?'

'I don't know. Just jump for Christ's sake.'

'You can bloody swim.' There had been panic in his voice. One or two of the other swimmers had glanced at him. She had moved her arms, treading water, and squinted up into the sun. 'For God's sake!'

'Stupid bitch.' He'd gritted his teeth in fear and leapt out over her head, trying to come down with his legs beneath him, gone under, emerged, found his feet and quickly waded off so that the water-level fell to his lower chest.

'I'm sorry,' she'd said later. 'I knew you'd be okay.'

'You can swim.' He'd rubbed oil on, not asking for help, and opened his book.

At half-past two the others returned. A couple of the men looked across at her as they passed to the stretch of beach they'd staked out earlier. She was lying on her back, her thighs slightly parted so that they didn't glue with sweat.

'I should imagine,' he told her, 'that they can see the roof of your mouth when you lie like that.'

'Fine.' She didn't open her eyes.

'You don't mind people peering straight up your snatch?'

'It's a bloody delight being on holiday with you.' She rolled over and wriggled a new declivity in the sand.

'I dreamed about my father last night.' He put his book down, letting the pages flap over in the breeze. 'Something about the war. There were guns firing. You know that Acropolis above the village . . . he was up there; I can't get the rest of it. I woke up with some sort of memory of something that had to be done urgently.' She didn't reply. 'It was very vivid. There was some sort of death-fear involved. I mean *I* was frightened of dying, but he was in the battle . . .'

'You're always frightened of dying.'

'What the hell does that mean? I was simply telling you . . .'

'The dog,' she said. 'It was so ridiculous.'

The dog plagued him. They had a room with a Greek couple high above the sea. Between the house and the first lane in to the village was a patch of scrub; donkeys grazed there and the boy who tended them had a dog. He'd marked it on the first day as they'd carried their bags up to the house; she'd seen his wary glance and had known what it would mean. Trips down to the beach and back again after the sun had lost its heat had been like running a gauntlet. The dog would bark at them and make little feinting runs down the slope towards the path. Each time, he strode yards ahead of her, arms rigid, his shoulders hunched.

'Dogs make me nervous,' he'd told her. 'Dogs in foreign countries I mean. Even if it hasn't got rabies – all right, it hasn't – you still have to go through the six-inch needles in the stomach routine. It takes a year to incubate, you know that, do you?'

That morning the dog had come at him, snapping and jumping. He'd swung the bag holding the water-bottle and books at it, yelling with fright, scrambling sideways down the hill until the boy had called it off. They still hadn't resolved the row they'd had about changing their room for one in the village.

He dug a shell out of the sand and lobbed it at the surf. 'I'm sorry you find me ridiculous.'

'It's only a puppy. You *are* ridiculous.'

'Jesus.' He stood up. 'What is that Greek arsehole doing?'

Manos had cast off the ropes that ran from the prow to the beach; the boat had swung sideways, wallowing slightly in the rising swell, tethered by its stern anchor only. They could see the fat figure standing on deck, yelling and beckoning. 'What the hell is he up to?'

The other passengers trooped past and began to get into the water. Manos lowered a rope ladder. The boat was well off-shore. Less than halfway there, those nearest had begun to swim.

'I don't fucking believe it.' He jabbed her with his foot and she sat up. 'The stupid bastard. Look. I can't get out there. Look.'

She stood up and gazed towards the boat. After a few seconds she began to put her bikini on. 'I'll go and tell him,' she said. He stood at the sea's edge while she waded in. As she began to swim, he looked along the beach and saw that it was empty of people. He walked into the sea until his bathing trunks were covered and stood there while she gained the boat and hung on to the lower rungs of the ladder. Manos leaned over to speak to her, his elbows resting on the rail, his forearms spreading and rising as he emphasized whatever it was he was telling her. The sea was distinctly choppy. Every now and then she'd be clouted by a wave and her hand would go up to wipe her face or push hair away from her eyes. Then she kicked off from the side of the boat and swam back.

'Well?'

'The sea's got up. He cast off because he wants to get going. He seems to think it's dangerous. He's anxious to go.'

'Terrific. That's wonderful.'

'The thing is – I think I ought to go back. All our stuff's on the boat: passports, money, travellers' cheques . . . everything. There's some arrangement with the taverna man. He'll drive you to the village. Don't you think that's best? Tell him what happened. Manos has got a deal with him; it's happened before. We could meet by the jetty. I mean, you're bound to be back before me.'

'All right.' He turned and waded back to the beach. 'Go on then.' He flapped a hand at her.

'Will you be okay?'

'You'd better go.' He sat down and shook the sand out of his plimsolls.

'Okay?' she asked again. She continued to look at him for a moment, then went deeper. He heard the splash as she started to swim.

It took him fifteen minutes to walk to the taverna. There were trestle tables set on a concrete verandah. They were still cluttered with the remnants of lunch, but no one was clearing them. The doors were locked. He knocked for a while, then walked round the place tapping at windows until he found the empty garage. Without looking further he backtracked to the verandah, took a half-full bottle of retsina from one of the tables and went out to the track that led to the village. They'd talked about walking to the beach earlier in the week; it was three miles, or so the locals said. The heat of the sun made his shoulders and back tingle. He took a swig from the bottle and started to walk. No one was there to see him or make him feel vulnerable in his trunks and plimsolls. A strange pleasure came on him, indivisible from malice. She would be back first, waiting at the jetty, wondering about him, knowing that she'd better stay put but having no notion of what had happened or where he was.

He drank off the wine and tossed the bottle against a rock. Everything was still and silent. The dirt road, white with dust, divided a steep, rocky hillside and sparse vineyards. A prickly green stubble sprouted here and there between boulders. The landscape was bleached and bare: no trees, no hedges, nothing to stop the eye but the brusque contours of the ground itself. He walked, looking from side to side at first, then letting his head

27

drop and falling into his thoughts. The landscape suited him; it was the kind of place he'd always thought of as compatible in his imaginings. He pictured his father jolting along the road in a camouflaged truck towing the thirteen-pounder. He was as in the photographs: young, handsome, wearing a slightly too large beret, his sleeves rolled up to where the chevron point of sergeant's stripes married with the straight crease in the khaki cotton. He began to describe it, working at the construction; then he caught a movement at the corner of his vision and turned to see the dog coming down the steep hillside, an awkward, spraddle-legged descent, its forelegs splayed to keep a balance, until it reached the road fifteen or twenty feet behind him, trotted forward and stopped. It looked directly at him, ears back.

He didn't move. The dog advanced in a crouch and stopped again. 'Go on!' He stamped a foot. 'Go on! Out of it!' The dog snaked a foot or so towards him. He turned his back and began to walk off and it was alongside, snapping, its teeth startlingly white against the black muzzle. 'Out of it!' He screamed the words, backing off. The dog paused, then ran at him again. Picking up a rock from the road he pitched it at the creature's front legs, making it scramble and retreat. Slowly, holding its stare, he crouched down and packed rocks into the crook of his left arm. When it rushed him again he started to throw.

He missed with the first. The second rock hit the dog square on its face between the ears. There was a crack, distinct and loud, like the sound made when a wishbone is pulled, and the dog stumbled and dropped a shoulder as its left leg folded; its muzzle scraped the dust; the entire forequarters seemed to tangle and slump. He threw again, taking it on the back directly over the spine. A triangle of skin tore off, making a dark, jagged smudge. The dog screamed and whipped round to nose the place but couldn't keep its balance and fell on to its side, still screwed into a circle. Then he threw rock after rock, advancing, thumping them into the black fur, into the snarling, half-lifted head. When he ran out of stones he gathered more, running to the verge and returning, aiming for the head and ribs. A sudden dark volley of blood squirted from the dog's nostrils. Bone was glistening on its brow where the fur had gone and its body was scabbed with wounds. It snarled and snatched at him but couldn't get up to attack. Finally, he straddled it and hurled the rocks straight down. Its hind legs bunched and flexed violently all the time as if it were trying to rise or run, and it gargled through its screams. When it voided its bowels he stood back and threw from a few paces away but it was as good as dead. He used his stones then left it and walked on.

After a mile he began to shake. In order to keep going he had to reach down and hold his left knee to give it strength. He thought that the sun must have burned his bare back and neck because his teeth were chattering and he felt lightheaded. He took ten minutes to rest, sitting in the shade of an olive tree just off the road. A tethered donkey was standing nearby, shaking its head ceaselessly to ward off flies. More than anything he wanted a drink and a cigarette and to be in the village among people. When he began to walk again he was picturing himself sitting beside her in their usual bar, drinking a cold beer and smoking a cigarette.

She was waiting on the jetty. As he approached, she got up and came to meet him. He could see that she was more worried than angry.

'What happened. I've . . .'

'You've been back for ages. Yes.' He put an edge of irritation into his tone. 'Taverna owner, he gone. Car gone. Place deserted.'

'You walked.'

'I walked.'

'Oh, Christ. Oh, look, the guy said . . . that bloody idiot!'

'Yes. Have you got the bags?'

She retrieved them from the jetty and dug out his T-shirt. 'I could use a drink.'

They walked past the telegraph office and the tiny shops selling lace and painted plates and past the restaurant with the

29

crenellated walls where they ate most evenings. The bar was in the last street before the lane that led up to their room.

'It was terrible,' she said. 'The bastard can't sail, to begin with. Add to that, his boat hasn't got a keel. We were all over the fucking ocean. One guy almost fell over the side. A woman lost her camera: that went full fathom five. Then one of the girls – the blonde one, freckles – she was sick and when she asked for water bloody Manos claimed not to have any. Then he stood at the wheel swigging Evian from a plastic bottle. The killer was, he made me pay for your trip back. I just paid up. I was imagining you waiting for me and wondering why we'd taken so long. Twenty-five drachs. He simply can't sail; he's hopeless. He stood there spinning the wheel, bloody cowboy, with his belly and his tortoiseshell cigarette-holder.'

'Manos drinks in here,' he said as they climbed the six steps into the bar. 'I'll find him later.' They sat down at a table on the verandah and lit cigarettes. 'Can you get the drinks?' he asked. 'I'd like two bottles of beer.'

'Yes, all right.' She pushed her chair back and stood up, then hung on to the rail for a second or two and closed her eyes. 'God,' she said. 'I can still feel the deck under my feet.'

THE THIRD YEAR

*

March

She did whorish things to him in bed – not to excite him or because she felt that way; she couldn't take pleasure in their lovemaking and she wanted it to be over with. He hated the loneliness of it all and the way she had become practised and sleazy.

He watched her at the stove: the smooth weight of her buttocks in the polished denim, how the thick seam ran between her legs, cinching her up. She turned, half facing him, dropping a shoulder. The overhang and curve upwards of her small breast was delineated against her T-shirt – its true shape. 'Do you want bacon as well?' she asked. 'There's some in the fridge.'

He fetched it and cut the packet open, then sat down to watch her again, picking up his drink and sighting her across the levelled rim of his glass. First he isolated her head, then took a bead on a point between her shoulder blades, then lowered the glass until it was almost at his lip and her backside sat on it, just above the level of the whisky. He felt immensely tired and knew that it was mostly due to the booze. Sometimes there were gaps in his recollection when he woke, like passages in a dream-narrative that won't come back however hard they're worked at, or elisions on a car radio when the car goes under a bridge. That, or he could remember events in their essence but not their particularity. It resembled, he supposed, the first touch of madness.

'How many rashers?' she asked.

'Three. Aren't you having anything?'

'Not fried stuff. You know that.'

'I didn't ask for a fry-up. We could have had anything.'

'I'm not hungry. I'll do this and go to bed. I've had a headache all day.'

'We could still go out to eat if you wanted to.'

'Oh, shit!' She stepped back, rubbing at her arm as the bacon crackled and spat. She poked at it from a distance looking resentful and amateurish.

'Let me do it.'

'Go and sit down for Christ's sake.'

He tried to take the spatula from her and she wrested it back. Droplets of grease flew from it and freckled the wall.

'For God's sake sit down!'

He went back to the drinks cupboard and poured more whisky into his glass. As he moved towards her, making for the tap, she screamed and stamped her foot.

'I just want some water. We *could* still go out if you'd like that.'

'I would like,' she gripped the spatula until it trembled in her hand, 'you to sit down while I finish this; then I would like to go to bed. Please stop hovering around . . . *looking* for things.'

'Looking for what?'

'Please!' She closed her eyes.

He looked at her face then turned away and took a swallow from his glass as he walked back to the chair. He thought: 'I'm drunk.' He almost said it out loud.

She shovelled the contents of the frying-pan on to a plate and took it to the table. 'Okay.' It wasn't a question; she said it as someone who has completed a task. She went to the television and switched it on for him, finding, by sheer luck, a mid-week football match. 'Okay,' she said again, 'I'm going to bed.'

He lifted his knife and fork then put them down. Without looking at her he said, 'Fried bread and fucking circuses. I see.' His words seemed to tangle with the football commentary.

'Look,' she was halfway out of the room; she spoke with her back to him, her hand pushing her hair back from her forehead and holding it bunched at the crown, 'I'll try and make it easy for you. I've got a headache; I've had a lousy day; I'm not brimming with happiness; I'm weary to my bones. Are you with me so far? I would like to go to bed. Now, does that last remark seem a logical extension of what preceded it? It does to me. I'm assuming you agree. So here I am, in the process of heading for the bedroom. All in all I'd be grateful if you would shut the fuck up, stop nagging at me and let me go. Okay? Fine.' She turned round a little too swiftly, as if expecting him to be immediately behind her. He hadn't moved. 'Fine,' she said again. 'Goodnight.'

He waited for ten minutes, then went to the bedroom door to spot her in the mirror above the dressing-table. From the door, the mirror gave a view of the entire room. She had taken all her clothes off save the T-shirt and was reaching up to put something away on the top shelf in the wardrobe. He thought it was a bracelet – she kept her jewellery boxes up there – but taunted himself with the notion that it was a letter or a secret keepsake. He marked the place, then entered the room.

'I'm sorry,' he said. 'I didn't mean this evening to . . . happen.'

'Okay.' She forced a smile. Her hands fluttered down to her crotch, then away again as if she'd realized that the gesture was defensive, or too obvious, or attractive. Once she'd done that he couldn't help but look at the neat scrub of hair: a narrow triangle; and once he'd started to look he couldn't look away. With his eyes fixed, he said: 'I'm a bit pissed.'

'I know.' She put her hands on her hips – an awkward, involuntary pose – kept them there for a moment and finally let them fall on either side of her body. It wasn't a gesture of resignation but it looked like that, so he was prompted to move towards her and link his arms round her waist. He thought he'd made a gain. She copied the motion, joining her fingers for a second or two at the small of his back; then she realized her mistake and broke the embrace, moving a step away from him.

'No, don't,' she said. He looked past her at the reflection of her half-naked body in the cheval glass by the bed. 'Don't. I just . . .' She moved to the dressing-table and stood in front of its mirror and started to uncap bottles. She plucked some pink and blue cotton-balls from a jar.

She smeared the area around her eyes with cream so that

35

eyeshadow and mascara and eyeliner muddied with the cleanser. He stood behind her as she wiped herself with the cotton-wool, her head tilted leftwards for the left eye, then to the right for the right eye. He put a finger, gently, into the diamond-shaped gap where her buttocks curved to join her thighs and drew it up along the crease. She leapt, half turning, flailing with one arm to block him and caught the glass he'd put down as he'd entered the room. It was as if she'd been stung.

Whisky poured out of the glass and ran across the lace cloth on the dressing-table and into the bristles of her hairbrush. She looked at him, then put her back to him, dropping her head to avoid her reflection and his. 'Please go away.' She said it three times, softly, each time with the same inflection. 'For my fault,' he said, 'for my fault, for my most grievous fault.'

'You evil bastard,' she whispered. 'Go away.'

He smirked and prodded her in the back with a forefinger. 'Tell me why you do it. There must be a reason. Fear? Hatred? Cowardice? . . . Contempt? What do you want me to do? *Expect* me to do? Who are you crying for?' He prodded her again and it put her off balance so that she staggered a little. 'Shit,' he said.

She crumpled the lace into a ball and scrubbed at the bristles of the hairbrush. He started to cry himself: the tears taking him by surprise. It gave her her chance and she brushed by him and got into bed. He hadn't moved; but looking up he saw her face reflected – vacant – her cheeks streaked with black, her hair still pushed behind her ears. She was looking down at the tiny tent her feet made under the eiderdown. In the sitting-room someone scored a late goal and the commentator bellowed over the noise of the crowd.

She said: 'It's not you. It's me. All right?'

'Terrific.' He used the heel of his hand to wipe at the tears. 'Oh good. That makes all the fucking difference.'

He left the house and got a few drinks at his local. After that he stayed in a cinema for an hour or so watching part of a film they'd seen together earlier in the week. It seemed that the same audience, the same spoilers, were there with him. In the row directly behind, someone was translating the dialogue into Spanish for his friend. All over the auditorium a mutter of conversation, like a swathe of smoke, rose towards the screen and dulled the soundtrack; heads were together in the dark. He swivelled to stare at the translator. Almost as if he'd been expecting it, the man stabbed a finger at his angry face and said *'Shush!'* The gesture was heavily aggressive. Its twisted logic shook him. He turned back, quickly, as if he'd been caught peeking at some private sight. Then he got up and walked rapidly towards the exit.

When he got home she was asleep. He threw his clothes on the floor and climbed in beside her without needing to switch on the light. Since he'd left, she had taken off the T-shirt.

He woke before she did. The curtains were drawn back. The sky was clear and gunmetal bright; the leaves on the big plane tree at the bottom of the garden were bright yellow and half filled the view. He waited for the alarm clock to wake her – or, at least, to make her open her eyes, acknowledge wakefulness. From time to time he glanced at her, disturbing in himself the notion that sleeping faces are supposed to provoke protectiveness. She looked as if she were listening to something: a proposition offered at a meeting or an argument that she'd already predicted and was ready to counter. The little declivity between her brows and slight pursing of the lips seemed contradictory and faintly censorious. When the alarm sounded, her expression relaxed.

She shut off the alarm and got out of bed at once. Crossing to the dressing-table, she looked at her face in the mirror. He watched. When she reached down, her hand struck the glass just as it had the previous night. This time she caught it with her knuckles, the motion extending to some other object, and it rapped against the wood and broke. In the instant that the glass fractured she screamed: stiff-legged with anger, the obscenities seamlessly joined in a single, unlikely vileness. It touched him like a hot wire. He vaulted from the bed, clearing the bed-rail, and slapped at her shoulders and face. She fought back, still yelling. Their heads collided, a flurry between them, until he caught her forearm and held it. She spat at him, hawking the stuff up from her throat, tugging to get away. He snatched the stem of the half-shattered remnant of the glass and, holding her hand as one holds a child's when it is to be punished, cut her alongside the thumb, between the joint and the knuckle of her first finger. They both stood still. Three or four beads of blood ran away from the sharp edge into the part-bowl of the glass. He let go. She looked at him, then at her hand, then back at his face again as she backed out of the bedroom holding the place. For a second she paused in the doorway and uncovered the wound, slowly, as if she were releasing a butterfly; then she clamped her palm back. Blood had dripped on to her thigh.

'Oh,' she said. 'Oh. Oh, dear Lord.' Her teeth were chattering. She sat down heavily in the passageway, then got to her feet after a minute or so, working her back upwards against the wall so as not to have to use her hands, and went into the sitting-room.

He lowered himself on to the bed, still holding the glass; then he laid it on the eiderdown and picked up his shoes from where he'd levered them off the night before. As he tugged at the knots, he heard the 'ping' of the telephone being lifted from its cradle.

THE THIRD YEAR

*

May

He said, 'I'm sorry, was I talking to myself again?' The words had been barely evident to him, but he'd caught her look and remembered something like, 'It can't . . .' and 'No, it's just . . .' The rest was a fleeting inner-ear impression of tone and delivery; he couldn't recall the sense. The fragments came back to him like driftwood recovered by the tide, their broken ends grimed, their original purpose lost.

'Yes, you were.' She bit into the piece of toast she'd just buttered and looked past the balcony railings to the casino: its fake Doric pillars and dead, neon calligraphy. It seemed likely to him that those truncated sentences were all he'd said – some censor acting to cut off the substance of whatever he might have meant. In any event, she gave him no lead. She was naked and sat at the plastic and alloy breakfast-table in a casual way, one thigh crossed loosely on the other, but not without a hint of tension, as if she hoped that her nakedness wouldn't move him. Three guests came out of the pool door and strolled across the astro-turf for a swim. He checked on the angle of their eyeline in relation to the balcony's concrete lip.

'Today . . .' she stood up and stretched, 'I thought we might drive to the inland sea.'

'Is it far?' He couldn't think why he'd asked. On the island, nothing was far. You could cross from side to side in less than half-an-hour. She went inside and fetched the map to show him, laying it over the cups and bowls and eggshells and tapping the place, her sprout of pubic hair level with his cheek. He nodded. 'Fine.' All maps seemed a maze to him. When he looked up she had gone to take her shower.

In the pool a girl in an orange bikini was howling and being ducked. He pondered the word 'antics' for what was going on.

The man was broad and dark. He wrapped a strong forearm around her nipped waist and swam backwards, holding her captive. The other man stood at the poolside waiting to dive. The girl called out a name and tried to hook his leg with her foot as she was hauled past – ignoring, for the moment, the man beneath her. She wanted them both in attendance. The diver broke his pose and squatted on his haunches to talk to his friends. He crouched so that one knee was fractionally lower than the other. His forearms lodged comfortably atop either thigh and his hands hung loosely, fingers relaxed. A small pendant or coin on a long chain swung out from the pelt on his chest and caught the sun.

They seemed to chat for a long time, as if something – some snag to the day's plans – had suddenly been discovered. The couple in the pool trod water, still linked by the man's thick arm. Of a sudden they all appeared oddly solemn. When the girl reached up and swept a waterlogged hank of blonde hair over her shoulder, the unstudied gesture appeared to attest to the seriousness of what they were saying. He watched them carefully but wasn't able to quarry the relationship out of their different situations. Finally, the swimmers separated and stroked sedately to the pool's rim, then hoisted themselves out; they spread towels on two loungers, dragged them round to face the sun, and lay on their backs. The other walked round to the diving-board, went to the end, bounced a few times, let the board settle, and shaped up for his dive.

'I'm ready.' He turned his head as she reappeared through the french windows and only heard the splash. When he looked back, the pool seemed empty; then the man's head appeared in a flurry of spray a full forty feet from the board. She folded the map and handed him the door key.

He drove out of the car park with his upper back wedged against the seat and his legs lifted away from the hot plastic: he was wearing shorts. After a while the slipstream cooled the car's interior. Her directions were flawless. She was the kind of traveller to whom you could say: 'Head south for three miles, then go due west until the road forks.' She'd know what to do. Instructions of that sort did nothing but conjure images for him. He saw hers as a utilitarian talent akin to the possession of perfect pitch. In places they'd never visited, she would steer towards an objective like someone who'd covered the ground before and bring him to their destination with an air of certainty that made it seem as though her arrival minutely preceded his. On occasions she'd say, 'Here we are,' as she might if guiding a first-time guest to a favourite weekend retreat.

She took them to a road built from ribbed concrete slabs, bordered on both sides by a token rim that gave on to a fifty-foot drop. Further up the hill on the driver's side, dumper trucks were dropping loads of garbage amid clouds of grey dust: backing up to the canyon's edge and letting the spillage go through the scrub and rocks. The cleft between them and the road was a partly filled pit of decaying refuse. Looking down he could see the solid horseshoe of water, apparently motionless, beneath a semicircle of sheer cliff.

When they got out of the car and began to walk downhill, the heat was so intense that he felt as if he were being buoyed up by it; his steps were light; his hair rustled like the roadside grasses. The massive fossil of the cliff held the air and boiled it. Trapped by its span, the acre or so of salt water, landlocked except for the tunnel that fed it, propelled tiny, crisp breakers on to the shingle. They sat on a groyne and put their feet in the little swell that ran along its side. Facing the strip of beach was a string of boat-houses so tiny that they looked more like bakers' ovens. Everything under the vast hang of bristly cliff was dwarfish.

There was a cave, its entrance draped with fishnet, where the rock tapered down to the shore. A wooden notice like a stunted signpost read: 'Wine ice-cream snacks'. Inside, in the cool semi-darkness, a girl of about fourteen stood beside a tall refrigerator. The floor was packed earth and stones, but someone had constructed a crude window at the back of the cave to provide some light and an access for the cables that ran the fridge. A table bore bread and platters of cheese under muslin.

He asked for two glasses of wine and she brought tumblers which she filled to the brim. They smiled at one another when she took the money. As he shouldered the netting aside, she stepped further back into the gloom. The glare outside was so great that she disappeared. He looked back for a moment and the girl was invisible, though he knew that she could see him through the lopsided diamonds of netting.

'It's like something remembered from a dream.' He nodded and gave her one of the drinks by reaching across her shoulder and settling it in her hand. She took the glass without looking. It tilted slightly and some of the wine spilled into the sea.

It had been a week and the island's oddities had begun to pall. The sun and the smiling people had begun to pall.

The previous day they had visited one of the monumental churches that crowded in to every view. Its nearest likely congregation lived in a fishing village four miles away; five hundred people could have attended mass without packing its pews. It was bare of decoration. One of the side chapels was walled with pegboard behind a wire lattice; it bore letters and offerings: each a token of gratitude for some miracle. A crash helmet, stove in on one side; a soiled bandage in a glass-fronted case; a dozen or so aluminium crutches; a truss; a baby's garments . . . Each votive remnant had next to it, alongside its letter, a photograph. They had made a slow circuit, laughing and shuddering.

Every evening they read the menu carefully, looking for a combination they hadn't yet tried; sometimes they ate on the terrace, sometimes in the restaurant itself. She noticed (but he didn't) that each time they chose the terrace he started his meal with soup.

The sun was almost masked by the cliff's crest. The hollows in the rock face were accreting pools of dim light, maroon becoming mauve and furry-edged. An hour or so before, a cranky little three-wheeled truck had arrived to fetch the girl and her supply of wine. She hadn't made a sale – apart from their repeat orders – all day. A young man had loaded the crates and the table; then he'd dragged the net aside, tying it back like a curtain in a suburban drawing-room. When the girl switched off the fridge, they became aware that they'd been able to hear its monotonal hum, on and off, for hours. The cliff's shadow enveloped her arms and she gave a tiny shiver. The water darkened a shade. Neither of them seemed inclined to make the move to leave. They had sunbathed throughout the day and read their books. The girl, with her supply of wine and sandwiches, had been their principal reason for staying: they'd expected the cove to be deserted, apart, maybe, from a visit by a group or two of tourists. In fact, no one else had come to look at the odd scene.

She marked her page by turning down its corner and lobbed the book into their shoulder-bag, but didn't stand up. She began to pick sand out from between her toes.

'We ought to get back.' He closed his own book and leaned over to rummage in the bag for car keys. Keeping his voice light, he asked, 'What did I say?'

She looked at him straight-faced. The look meant, *Go on* . . .

'When I realized I was talking to myself. This morning. I wondered what I'd said.' She shrugged and shook her head. 'Doesn't matter, or didn't hear?' he asked.

'Didn't hear.' She dusted her toes and held each foot above the ground in order to keep them sand-free as she put on her sneakers. '*You* heard *me*, though.'

'Yes,' he said. She had risen at about five o'clock that morning and had gone out to the balcony where she'd stayed for an hour or more, smoking cigarettes. It had taken her quite a while to wake from the nightmare. She'd been restless and he'd assumed that she was unable to sleep. Then she'd begun to mutter and move from one shoulder and flank to the other. A hand had flopped into his face just as he was beginning to doze and looking over he'd seen, in the thin silver light from the balcony windows, that the other had been clawing the air. After she had come awake she'd taken her cigarettes from the bedside table and gone out immediately, treading quietly and closing the window when the net curtain had begun to billow.

She shuffled backwards out of the shade, drawing her knees up and extending them by turns in a rowing action. Rooting around by the breakwater, earlier, she'd found him a good pebble: a smooth quartz with a reddish-brown area like a blush or a bruise. Stooping with her knees under her chin, she held it out to him, extending her arm fully behind her own line of vision. He polished it on his shorts and looked at the damp kink in her hair where it gathered at the nape of her neck.

'Was it much?'

'No. I mean no creatures from Hieronymus Bosch or leaden-booted efforts to escape a forest fire. It had . . . it came from something . . . I mean I realized more or less at once what it was.' She had dug a shell out of the sand and was using it to make little formal patterns on the flesh of her thigh. 'Just before we came away – the day before – I was driving to the junction by the supermarket and I'd got into the wrong lane, so I signalled and crossed to the left. There was some guy too close to be seen in my wing-mirror and I almost hit him: I guess he must have had to brake pretty sharply. Anyway, I'd cut him up. He hooted and so on and swerved over to my right. I ought to have seen him I suppose. Anyway, we pulled up at the light next to one another. I looked across to deliver a foolish-grin-and-wide-eyed apologetic routine. He was waiting for me to look. He made this sort of . . . gesture; not fingers: you know; it was . . . he made a fist and kept his forearm straight and sort of slowly worked it up past the window – slowly – and twisted it as he raised it. It was horrible; I mean, I could . . . it made my knees weak. I couldn't look away. I can't imagine what was on my face. He did it twice – as if I hadn't read it the *first* time – so that his elbow was up to the sill. He wanted me to understand that he meant deep. Then he did this –' she drew a finger across her throat: not just a horizontal, cutting motion, but an extravagant, dragging semicircle from the lobe of her left ear to that of her right, coming under her Adam's apple at its lowest point and almost into the declivity between her collar-bones, pressing so that the finger seemed to meet resistance. She shivered again. 'It actually made me afraid.'

He coughed, shaking his head. 'What then?'

'Oh, we drove off. He didn't follow or anything – I watched in the mirror. I don't mean that sort of frightened.'

'It's odd that you should be so upset by it.' He polished the pebble. 'I mean, you're not one to use sex to mollify or console, if you see –'

'It was just – it wasn't simply one of those insulting gestures.' She hesitated. 'It was for me. Invented for the occasion.' She laughed at the notion, then fell silent. She didn't tell him about the dream.

The sky was still bright but there was no sun, now, on the dinky beach. He saw that they had forgotten to return one of the glasses: it was standing on the end of the groyne, so he took it to the cave's entrance and set it down on a rock, putting a stone inside to fix it there. He walked back across the trim segment of shingle, tiny charges of aggression and worry nipping at him like a weak, intermittent voltage: similar to the distress he sometimes felt when he recalled that something was perturbing him but couldn't bring it to mind.

When he took his place beside her on the sand, she remarked how the bowls of shadow on the cliff were deepening: purple and rust, opaque, like the bloom on a plum. It seemed their soft light settled on the retina – the onset of blindness. Together they sat and watched, each preserving the effect as a memory of the place.

THE THIRD YEAR

*

July

Because there was nothing much else to do they ordered all four courses at lunch. The wine was free and there was a good deal of it. On all sides the French bourgeoisie clattered and chewed and indulged its children.

'It's the big event of the week,' she said. 'All mealtimes are sacrosanct, but Sunday lunch particularly. Are the soft-shelled crabs okay?'

'They appear to be full of black sludge.' He filled their glasses, drank half of his and topped it up again. 'I think this must qualify as the most exquisitely boring town I've ever visited.'

The lamb arrived and more wine. 'We'll go back to that antique shop.' She looked at him for a reaction. 'Where the woman had that odd dog.'

'Pharaoh hound.'

'Right. I want to look at that bowl again.'

'How much was she asking for it?'

'We didn't get round to that. I do wish you spoke French. I have to do all the bargaining. It's better if a man does it. Don't drink all of that.'

'It's free.'

'All the more reason not to feel obliged to finish it.'

'It depends how you look at things. Christ, don't nag.'

'I just don't want you to get pissed.'

'I see.'

'Okay. All right.' She held up a hand, palm out, her head bowed in mock deference, then picked up her knife and cut into the meat. 'You're not going to like the lamb.'

He peered at his plate. A runnel of pink blood was travelling round the rim, making little oxbows where it met islands of grease in the gravy.

'It's paid for,' he said. 'I can leave it.' He smoked a cigarette while she ate, and drank a few more glasses of wine. When they emerged she was drunk enough to be slurring her speech.

Their car was parked in the town square, close to the antique shop. The Pharaoh hound lay outside by the array of china and furniture, one paw crossed foppishly on the other, the bony face immobile. He stood close to it, feigning indifference, while she handled the bowl, passing her palms across its polished oval surfaces, examining the joins and mends. The woman who owned the shop stood at her shoulder murmuring encouragement.

'It's two hundred francs,' she said, without looking at him.

'What would you do with it?'

'I don't know.' The consonants slopped into each other. 'Fruit, I suppose. It was a cream bowl.'

The woman caught a word and took the bowl from her, holding it between the crook of her arm and her breast. 'La crème,' she affirmed, making a whipping motion inside the bowl with her free hand.

'Ah, oui.' He smiled. 'Buy it then, if you want to.'

'We could come back this way.' She spoke a dozen or so words to the woman then turned stumbling against a small stool before getting through the door. The dog got up and yawned, lowering its jaw and raising its rump so that the rill of backbone seemed to flow under the taut grey coat. Then it growled absentmindedly at them.

'What were they used for?' She tossed the keys to him across the car roof.

'Hunting.'

'What?'

'I don't know. Israelites, I expect. Do you really want to come back?'

'Possibly. It's on the way – if we want it to be. Let's just drive for a bit. I'll think about it.'

'We can easily afford two hundred.'

'I know,' she said. 'It's no great hardship to come back.' He started the car and drove to the town limits. 'Where to?'

'I don't know. I'm too pissed to make much sense of the map. Just drive for a bit. We can't get lost. Keep circling.'

'All right,' he said. 'Don't go to sleep.'

It had rained more or less persistently. They woke, most mornings, to the sound of rain in the trees outside the house; when they looked out the countryside would be occluded by a blue-grey rain-mist. Each day he trudged a mile into the village for eggs and milk. The woman who sold them to him had a few words of English.

'Toujours, toujours . . . it is bad to be always rain.' She would raise a hand towards the roof while ladling the milk. 'For the grapes it is bad.'

'Will the wine be poor this year?' He'd chopped the question into three in order to be understood.

'Yes, it will be bad.' She had nodded. 'No one can remember such rain. Now it is always sun here.'

He would get back to find her still in bed, reading. They spent mornings talking about driving further south, but never made any decision.

She dozed for twenty minutes then woke, clacking her tongue against the roof of her mouth. He took his flask from the map compartment in the door and passed it to her. 'You'd better have a livener.'

'Where are we?' She sipped some brandy and screwed the metal cap back on.

'Not sure. Take a look at the map. I think we've been driving due west.'

She peered out at the dense woodland on both sides of the road. 'Stop for a moment,' she said, unfolding the map. 'I'll try to work it out.'

He pulled off the road on to a track between the trees and took out his cigarettes while she angled the map to try to fix the place.

'Any good?'

'Yes, I know roughly where we are. You didn't exactly circle.'

She smeared some of the condensation off her side-window. 'It's almost stopped raining,' she said. 'Miracle of miracles.'

'It hasn't been *too* dreadful, has it?' He leant over and kissed her. 'One or two problems, but . . .'

'No.' She kissed him back. 'No, fine.' He would never have been able to predict what she next did. She took his hand and laid it over her breast: an instruction; and turned towards him in her seat, making things easier. He felt elated. He tried to get the pace right so as not to annoy her or disrupt the moment.

'I think it would be easier outside.' She laughed; she seemed genuinely happy and lusty. 'Bring the blanket.'

He spread the blanket on the wet grass next to her door and she shuffled off the seat and on to the plaid wool without hitching up her trousers. In the car he had pulled them down to her knees. When he lay alongside her he worked them down to her ankles and raised her T-shirt over her breasts. Her kisses were fervent; she closed her eyes to deliver them.

She reached down to squeeze him and fumbled at his zip. Then she gasped and sat up quickly, looking over his shoulder. He was aware that her legs had banged against him. When he turned he saw why.

Two men were backing away to be out of reach, but not retreating. One was holding the trousers he'd yanked from her ankles. There was a livid green light in the wood; he noted it, and the sound of water dripping through the leaf canopy. The two figures were stark, side by side, watching them, back-lit by the weird glow. One of them stepped forward and laughed and shook her trousers and took a pace backwards to stand by his friend again.

'Who are they?' He stood up.

'What?' Not taking her eyes off the men, she eased her T-shirt down to cover her breasts and stood up too. She tweaked the elastic waistband of her knickers, pulling it upwards, and left her hand there to cover the dark shadow of her bush under the material.

'What did he say?'

They knew it would be a mistake to try for the car. The man with the trousers raised them to his face and sniffed the crotch. Then he spoke and passed them to his friend, who did the same.

'What did he say?'

'Oh Christ.' She stepped back, stumbling slightly, and gripped his wrist. He was grinding his teeth; a burning started in his stomach.

'I can't understand what they're saying. What should we do?'

Her face had lost its colour. She made little treading motions with her feet, like a cat kneading, as she watched the two men and listened to them.

'Try to tell me what they're saying. They look like gypsies. What did they say about your trousers?'

'Just . . . it was just dirty talk.'

'And now?'

'They're talking about who's going to go first.'

The two men were laughing and looking at them. One tossed the trousers aside and called out. He caught the word 'gazelle'.

'What was that?'

'A graphic description of how much I'm going to enjoy it.' He could feel her trembling through his wrist-bone.

'Tell them I'll kill them.' As soon as he'd spoken he laughed; it seemed so ludicrous to be asking her to translate something like that.

'Don't be fucking stupid.'

'Tell them.' He laughed again, but for emphasis shook the arm she was holding.

'It'll be worse – to start talking to them.'

'No. I'm trying to think. Tell them what I said.'

She called out and the men listened. Then they cackled with laughter. He laughed with them: an echo. He felt excited and reckless. 'Tell them again,' he insisted. 'I'll kill both of them.' He chortled helplessly through the words, like someone enjoying his own joke too much to be able to deliver the punch-line.

Suddenly, one of the men made a run towards them, passing in front and grabbing at her. For a moment the man held her by the arms, pulling her away from the car. She screamed and grabbed at the open door. The man ducked a punch, turned her round, and slapped her hard across the buttocks. Then he ran out of reach. There was a hush; another confrontation. She had started to cry when the gypsy grabbed her and now she couldn't stop.

'Don't get into the car.' He anticipated her. 'They'll close in if they think we're going to make a run for it. Just open the door wider.' She swung the door back and he stooped without looking back, reaching into the map compartment and coming up with a big, wooden-handled craft knife. He opened the blade, then twisted the metal ferrule to lock it into place. The men watched him. He held the knife out at arm's length and showed it to them.

'Tell them I'll kill them,' he ordered. 'Say it to them again.'

She started the message, coughed, began to cry harder. 'Shout it,' he told her. The gypsies listened. They looked serious, as if, somehow, they had been affronted. They moved forward, separating and circling, one coming towards the knife, the other moving rather faster in the direction of the car's boot. He knew what they were doing. When the faster man got to her and she screamed, he didn't turn. Instead, he stepped forward to meet the other's extended arm and stabbed hard, pushing the blade along and down, cutting him from wrist to elbow. The gypsy roared and sat down clutching at the wound.

The other man was holding her by the hair. He'd managed to get her knickers into a rope around the tops of her thighs. She was fighting in an awkward, ungainly way, her buttocks, white against the tan, jiggling as she attempted to kick and wrench herself away. The man released her when he heard the roar, and ran across to his friend.

Still holding the knife in front of him, he backed to where she stood, took her arm, and pulled her to the far side of the car.

'Get in the back seat,' he said. He followed her in and started the engine. The two gypsies looked up at him through the open door. The man he'd cut was holding his arm tightly and groaning. There was a lot of blood: on his arm, his fingers, on the top of his trousers. The second man crouched by him. Neither made any move as he reversed down the track and back onto the road.

He drove steadily for a mile or so without speaking. Finally he said, 'You'd better come into the front; I don't know where the fuck I'm going.'

She studied the map. 'Right at the next crossroads,' she said.

'Will that take us back to the town?'

'Yes.' She pulled his jacket off the back seat and spread it over her lap and naked legs. 'Was he badly hurt?'

'I think so. I must have hit something major.'

'He was bleeding a lot.'

'Yes.'

She started to cry again. 'It was so awful,' she said.

'Yes. Let's hope he dies.'

'Will there be trouble, do you think?' Her voice was plaintive and very soft. She waited to be advised.

'Don't be silly.'

She used the sleeve of his jacket to wipe her face and took a packet of cigarettes out of the glove compartment, but she couldn't get one lit. 'It was so awful.' Her head went on to her knees and she sobbed.

He parked the car in the same spot as before and went into the antique shop. After five minutes or so, she saw him running back through the rain, carrying the bowl under one arm. She unlocked the door and he got in, putting the bowl in her lap.

'I knocked her down by twenty-five francs.' He looked pleased with himself. 'She told me this wonderful story. It seems that the women of the house would use a bowl like this to hold a note for them when they sang. One of them would put a coin in the bowl, clutch it against her body with her arm round it and make a kind of swirling motion with her hip and waist. The coin would circle the bowl like a wall-of-death rider and give out a sort of drone. The women would pick up the note – as if it were a tuning fork. The serving-women and cooks and so forth. We ought to try it out later.'

'I know,' she said. 'She told me the same story.'

'Oh.' He was peeved. 'Perhaps it's part of the sales technique, then.'

'Perhaps. How was she able to tell you all this? How did you understand her?'

'It turned out that she speaks pretty good English. She asked where you were.'

'What did you say?' There was something akin to fear in her voice.

'That you were waiting in the car.'

'Did she ask whether I was ill or anything?'

'No. Why should she?'

'No. I don't know what I meant.'

She turned and put the bowl on the back seat, then tucked his jacket tightly under her thighs. The roads were deserted.

'I know my way home from here,' he told her. 'We're virtually on home ground.'

'His name was Alain,' she said.

'Which?'

'The one you cut. The one who hit me on the bottom.'

'How do you know?'

'The other one called him that.' She picked at a loose flake of plastic on the dashboard. 'I wish I didn't know his name,' she said. 'It's so awful to have to know his name.'

'Perhaps a centime isn't what it was.'

'You could be right.' She tried again, holding the bowl low against her hip, her forearm wrapped round its edge while she swung her torso outward and round. The coin scraped against the wood, rising and falling but not travelling along whatever line was needed to produce a sustained sound. When she quickened the swing of her hip, the coin hopped over the bowl's rim and skittered out of sight among chairlegs. She got on to her hands and knees and began to feel for it.

58

'I got a reduction,' she said, 'did I tell you that?'

He smiled. 'No. I thought she might knock a few francs off.'

'It was nice of you to drive back there. I'm sorry I went to sleep.'

'I knew you really wanted it; you couldn't decide because you were pissed.'

'I was, wasn't I? Where did we go?'

'You didn't miss much. I just drove a circle: for about an hour. I only got lost once. I was quite pleased.'

She found the coin and dropped it into the bowl. 'Did I really sleep for an hour?'

'More or less,' he said.

'Where did you go?' She twirled again, holding the bowl a little higher. The coin made half a circuit, then rattled into the base.

'It was countryside – woods and fields, sometimes a farm. We passed a gypsy encampment on the way back. A Citroën cut me up because I didn't know which road to take. Really, there wasn't anything much to see.'

She trapped the coin with the index finger of her free hand, fixing it half-way up the side, then, as she began to move, ran it against the motion as a croupier will with a roulette ball. It didn't take.

'I think,' he said, 'that you're supposed to be broad of hip and thick of arm; there's not enough of the peasant in you.'

'Why don't you try?' she suggested. 'Your lineage is choc-a-bloc with cooks, parlourmaids and tweenies, isn't that right?'

'True,' he replied, 'but there's bound to be some sort of ill-luck associated with a man doing it, wouldn't you think? The crops would fail, or something. The cows would go dry. We oughtn't to risk it.'

She had put her tongue out at him and exaggerated the gesture as he spoke. He laughed, crossing the room to get to the stove. 'Tea for madame?' he asked, and filled the kettle.

She persisted, losing the coin now and then, shifting the height of the bowl or changing the angle until, finally, it came

59

right. Her hips found whatever track it was that the bowl's shape required – a mildly obscene, ovoid line that made her look as if she were winding up for a bump and grind. The coin travelled two inches or so below the rim, drawing a low note, and she rose on to the balls of her feet to take it faster. The pitch lifted until a high drone filled the room. He watched the creases in her T-shirt switching left to right as one hip flung out, then the other – as her pelvis rocked to and fro. She was looking down, fascinated, at the coin playing solo in the bowl.

THE THIRD YEAR

*

September

'We're giving you Mrs Sims.' Geoff Cottrell approached, his hand cupped under the elbow of a woman in corduroys and a well-cut, fawn tweed blouson. 'Mrs Sims,' he said again as they both stopped a few feet away, and gestured with his free hand to make the introduction. Then he left to take his place among the leaders.

She smiled as they shook hands. 'I'm not at all sure what I'm supposed to do, you know.' The heavy stick, dog-legged like a riding crop, hung from the crook of one elbow. 'I mean, when to . . . quite how to *behave*.'

'Well, basically you kill for me. What I bring down but don't quite polish off, you knock on the head –' he pointed, 'with that.'

'Yes.' She unshipped the club and made a clumsy job of hefting it. 'But there are all sorts of things, aren't there, to do with not getting in front of the gun and so on?'

He grinned at her. 'I shouldn't worry too much. I'm tail-end Charlie, here. I'm not the best of shots. We're both tucked out of the way – where we can't do much damage.'

'Do you mind?'

'No, no. Geoff's doing the right thing. I'm really not too good a shot.'

'I didn't mean that.' She raised a hand skywards. 'Killing the birds, I mean.'

'Oh.' He shifted the gun from his left arm to his right. 'No. It's usual, isn't it? The farmers and the rest.'

She didn't reply immediately then said, 'No. I don't mind either.' She turned so that she was standing beside him looking out over the three acres of rough turf bordered by woodland. There were lines of frost on the tops of the grown-over furrows.

Ahead of them there was some activity: a deployment of guns. Three Land-Rovers were parked by the gate that led into the field, each carrying hampers, spare guns and cartridges.

'We aren't given a dog?'

'No,' he replied, 'a dog is only useful if you know it. Know how to work with it. It has to be your dog, really.'

'I see.' She looked a little rueful. 'When does it start?'

Mostly, he caught the loose stuff; or, at least, some of it. For the first fifteen minutes everything was out of kilter, then he began to find an eye. Mrs Sims did as she was bidden, trotting off to the downed birds, dispatching the maimed, and trotting back to deposit them in the bag. She had a curiously amateurish but touching habit of bundling the bodies against her chest and supporting them with bent arms, as if she were carrying a pile of books or a paper bag full of groceries. Just before lunch she rounded up three that had come over in quick succession. He'd missed two others, but was feeling pleased.

'I'm afraid this one's head came off when I bashed it.' On her cheek was a stripe of blood trapping a tiny curl of down. 'I am sorry. Is it terribly infra dig?'

He laughed at her eagerness. 'I don't know. Probably. Stuff it down to the bottom of the bag.' He raised the gun and she leapt sideways, but the bird was over and gone.

'I'm sorry. I put you off.'

'It doesn't matter. You're doing incredibly well. Are you cold?'

'Oh, no.' She said it quickly like a child who has been asked if it's tired. Her jacket was unzipped now, and there were spots of blood in the wisps of wool on the white angora sweater she was wearing underneath. He noticed that she had small, rounded breasts; they flattened and bounced as she brushed at the stains.

'There's some here.' He teased off the down, leaving a pattern on her cheek, and rubbed with his thumb, making the mark paler but bigger. She stood still, her arms held loosely downwards, and cocked her head to let him get at the place. 'I've made

64

a bit of a mess.' She smiled and weighed the bag with her hand, letting it drop between them. 'We haven't done *too* badly, have we?'

At lunch they sat on the tailgate of one of the Land-Rovers and joined in with the chatter. 'When I arrived . . .' she smeared a wedge of pork-pie with mustard from a tube and held it in front of her mouth for when she'd finished talking, 'the servant – the girl who came up to my room and unpacked – said she couldn't find my clothes-cover.'

'What? I mean, what is it?' He was sitting close to Geoff Cottrell, so he lowered his voice. She chuckled and touched his arm conspiratorially. 'I didn't know. I acted as if I did and said I must have forgotten to pack it. So she brought me one.'

'And –?'

She bit into the pie and pushed a crumb into the corner of her mouth with a finger. 'Well . . .' A pause, while she chewed long enough to be able to speak. There was an easiness between them, something casual, chummily intimate, that had grown out of their morning's teamwork. 'It's – it turned out to be an oblong of rather ornate, embroidered brocade with a sort of fringe – well, yes, a fringe – that they put over your knickers and bra and so on when they lay out your clothes. In the morning, or before dinner, you know. I imagine that it's some sort of safeguard against attacks of unbridled lust that might be provoked in any manservant coming into a lady's bedroom to switch on the light over the old master or to heave a tree trunk into the grate.' She giggled: then, as if the notion had struck her fully for the first time, started to laugh full-bloodedly. One or two of the others looked up, smiling involuntarily, wondering what the joke was. He laughed too, more at her laughter than at what had been said. When she realized she was being looked at she grew selfconscious, but the shape of the laugh stayed on her face as if she were too embarrassed to re-compose it abruptly. The people nearby stopped talking. She lowered her head and blushed. He passed her a long-stemmed glass full of wine to give her something to do and thought of a question to ask. When everyone had started talking again she drank the wine.

They stopped at about three-thirty. He was cold and had a headache from the gun. Mrs Sims had said little after lunch. She'd stayed close, doing her work well; and once or twice he'd felt her looking at him. He broke the gun when he saw Geoff Cottrell waving and making a move towards the Land-Rovers.

'I think we're going,' he said.

She walked towards him, flapping her arms across her chest. 'I can't say I'm sorry.'

He smiled at her. 'Had enough, have you?'

'No.' There was a lift in her voice; she didn't want to appear ungracious. 'No, it's just so cold. A bath and a drink . . .'

'To tell the truth,' he said, ejecting the two unused cartridges, 'I haven't been able to feel my feet for half an hour. I'm not at all sorry either.'

They travelled back in the same Land-Rover, but sat at different ends: she nearer the driver. He glanced at her once and she was waiting for it. They exchanged smiles, then she lowered her eyes. Geoff Cottrell passed him a flask and asked if he'd had a reasonable day. 'Terrific,' he said. 'Wish I could hit more of them.' Cottrell laughed. When he looked at her again she was talking to one of the other women, holding the crooked stick between finger and thumb so that it dangled near her knees and tapped against the rim of the bench seat.

His being away made space, made a space in the bed and in each room, space in her life for things they couldn't comfortably share. It sometimes occurred to her that she ought, during one of his absences, to give a party for the friends he hated, at which they would play the music that only he couldn't bear to hear and eat the food he found repellent. Who could say what such contrariness might lead to? She put a record on – something she'd owned for ten years or more – then made herself a weak drink. She pictured him and chuckled. It was probable, she realized, that he was in the company of people he thought pompous and stupid, having food

served to him that he disliked. She couldn't remember much about
Geoff's or Molly's taste in music. Chopin under the rattle of ice in
glasses perhaps; or Simon and Garfunkel.

She had made some trivial plans. Three days and five nights;
one night and most of the first day gone. She would keep her
own company for most of the time: read, catch up on some work,
use the space. Excursions with the dog, gardening . . . There
was a movie she wanted to see on her own. She'd had a call, two
days before he'd left, from an ex-boyfriend who had gone to live
abroad – someone who might have become a friend in different
circumstances. A drink maybe, or dinner; a trading of recollections and names. She wondered whether the phone might ring:
what he was doing.

Steam fogged the mirror. He lowered himself on to his hands
and knees until his skin became accustomed to the temperature
of the water, then levered his body backwards into a crouch and
stayed like that for a few more minutes before sitting down,
inch by inch, finally leaning backwards, gasping, so that the
water all but covered his chest. He unfocused and relaxed; then,
without at all meaning to, began to rehearse a duologue.

' . . . It was fine. You know how you never lack for anything
down there. They put me in our usual room. Collins dashed
about like a blue-arsed fly, running baths and laying out dinner-
jackets. Geoff was admiring of the gun but still had the good
sense to put me at the back of the field.'

He put her by the sink, shredding lettuce and dropping it into
a sieve. She was wearing jeans and a Guernsey. 'Did you bag
much?' she asked. She'd say 'bag' in an amused way; not
meaning to sound unkind though.

'More than usual, actually. I had a Mrs Sims.'

'Are you going to make the dressing?' She reached out and
ran one of the taps, but he couldn't devise what for.

'You know . . .' he opened a high cupboard and took out the
oil, vinegar and mustard, ' . . . to wallop the lame and halt over
the head.'

'Not nice.' She wrinkled her nose and shook drops of water from her fingertips. 'How was Molly?'

'Fine. Ruthlessly efficient, as always. Pregnant.'

'What, again?'

'They seemed pleased.' He passed behind her for some reason and patted her bottom. She moved so that he managed only one pat, and went to the table with knives and forks, salt and pepper.

'Mrs Sims seemed a bit odd to me.' He could hear the teaspoon grating against the rough surface of the pottery bowl as he melded the oil and vinegar. 'Not eccentric or anything.' He gave himself time to work out what he wanted to say. 'She seemed preoccupied with deciding how best to behave.'

'Well, Geoff and Molly do know some pretty odd people. Remember that Bennett man.' She said that quickly as she lit the candles, then stepped away from the table. He could see the anger in her pose: the way she regarded the place-settings. 'Are they just going to keep on breeding for ever?' she asked.

At dinner, Mrs Sims sat opposite him and one place to his left. She was wearing a dark dress, cut square at the neck and set off by a line of green embroidery. It looked oddly childish, except when she leaned forward to get the sauce-boat or to stub out her cigarette; then a tip of cleavage would appear, and a slight, freckled chubbiness that was the very upper slope of her breast. She'd drawn her hair back with a tortoiseshell comb. Tiny diamond studs decorated her earlobes.

When she wasn't eating she smoked. The man on her right chatted to her for a while, then dutifully switched his attention to his own right-hand side when the fish was served. The man to her left shifted his weight and spoke and she responded with a smile, saying that she hadn't quite caught his remark, but he was talking to the woman on his other side: he'd only turned in order to reach the bread-basket. She blushed and made an awkward gesture, inadvertently putting her hand into her food. As he watched her she wiped her fingers on her napkin, then

68

drained the wine in her glass and muttered something to herself. When she took a cigarette from her case, he lobbed a box of matches across the table. She fielded it as it skittered on the cloth. She didn't look up at him at all, or throw the box back when she'd taken a match out and lit up.

The meal was almost ended before he got a response. She'd been leaning slightly forward, her torso bowed, chin on hands; it was a pose that effectively excluded the men on either side without being extreme or attention-getting. As if emerging from thought, she reached back and took her handbag off the rail of her chair, opened it, extracted a pen and something to write on and, after scribbling a message, flipped it towards him like someone dealing a playing-card. It was a photograph of a child – taken, it seemed, at Christmas-time. On the floor were toys and a litter of rumpled wrapping paper. The child, a boy, was looking straight at the camera: sitting cross-legged amid the debris, a teddy bear on his lap. He was smiling a false, obliging smile. Presumably it had been all she'd had to write on. On the back she'd put: *Bored to death! Feel like a walk?*

Between the acre or so of lawn and the hedges that bordered the flower-garden was a broad, gravelled path. They walked along it, looking back at the house. Elegant shapes bloomed and receded in the tall windows as people fetched coffee or a *digestif*. She billowed smoke and frosted breath, dropping the stub on to the grass and arranging her shawl in the crook of an elbow so that she could link her arm, loosely, through his. A light came on under the eaves.

'Someone's turning down my bed,' she remarked.

'What?' He followed her upward gaze.

'That's my room; there – the middle one where the light's just been switched on.'

As they watched, someone inside half closed the curtains. After a second or two the light went out. 'I'm in the Blue Room,' she said; then, as if looking for a reason for having offered the information, 'I don't think I've ever slept in a room with a *name* before.' They stood still, looking up at the darkened window, until he thought to ask her whether she knew Geoff Cottrell well and they could continue their stroll back down the path and alongside the lawn towards the french windows.

'Thanks.' She smiled and detached her arm as they stepped into the pool of light. He followed her in, meaning to get her some coffee, but she went directly across the room and left by the door that opened on to the hall. Moving as if it had been his intention all along, he turned to the table that bore the coffee and liqueurs and poured himself a brandy. The guests had thinned out: just a few drinkers bringing down their birds for the fourth or fifth time. He drank the brandy, poured himself another, and left them to it.

As he undressed, sounds filtered through to him of the household settling for the night. It had been after midnight when he'd got to his room. He'd decided to leave it until a quarter to one. He read, sipping the brandy he'd brought up with him. He felt gloomy, just as he had all day. It was a portent: in him, melancholy often led to some rashness. Briefly, he wished he possessed the talent for action without analysis – the pure pleasure of mindlessness. Sometimes even the simplest movement plagued him. Emptying a rubbish-bin, removing his glasses to rub his eyes, opening a door . . . He couldn't perform the motions without being conscious of having provoked the motor responses that dictated them. He saw the cortex as a cable of filigree wires buzzing with messages: scratch, lift, retreat, step up, remove, turn, observe.

It hadn't been necessary to chart her room from the position of the window. The Blue Room had a blue door, it was as simple as that. It seemed to be locked, but when he twisted the knob the other way the door opened. The dressing-table light was on. At first he thought she had gone to sleep, waiting. She was propped up on pillows, not moving, breathing deeply. From just inside the door he viewed her in profile; but her eyes were open. He whispered and she drew her knees up under the coverlet, wrapping her arms round them, contriving to look straight ahead.

He walked to the side of the bed and laid a hand on the cuff of the turned-back sheet. She moved her shoulders forward as if to shift the bedclothes and let him in; but she moved back again, then forward, then back, rocking with her knees hugged to her chest. The motion grew more pronounced. Her hair fell across her cheek, then back; the coverlet began to slip. 'Poor,' she said. 'Poor. Poor. Poor. Poor. Poor.' Her voice was surprisingly loud.

He tried to stop the rocking by putting the flat of his hand against her shoulder. She strained against him for a moment before slumping back as if she were giving up. He drew the covers right back. She was wearing a peach-coloured nightgown with scallops of lace at the bodice. He lifted it from the hem. She kept her knees and ankles together. He rested his hand on the furze where her thighs joined and tried to get a finger underneath. She didn't yield, so he put a hand on each of her knees and started to draw her legs apart, getting up on to the edge of the bed.

As he crossed her line of vision she seemed to come awake or notice him properly for the first time. She gasped and her eyes dropped to her own white torso and legs. Her hands went out to the ruck of her nightgown bundled across her ribs, and she drew it up a little as if to get a better sight of herself; then she looked at him again and her mouth opened. For an instant there was no sound. Then she went, 'Ah!' – a sharp, single syllable, the noise a parent makes when admonishing a child who is about to do something wrong. 'Ah!' she said again.

He put a knee between her thighs and leaned over her, stiff-armed, resting on his palms. 'Ah!' she said. 'Poor! Poor!' – so loudly that she was almost yelling. Raising herself on her elbows, she put her face close to his. 'Poor!' She bellowed it. 'Poor! Poor! Poor!'

Doors were opening in the hallway. He heard a man say something and a woman's sharp, capable reply. Beneath him she was showing her teeth; her hair was hanging back from her scalp. 'Poor!' she roared. 'Poor! Poor!' Without shifting her position she began to cry noisily. There was a knock at the door. A voice asked her if she were all right. Neither of them moved or responded. A second voice asked the same question. There was another knock. She had stopped crying as suddenly as she'd begun.

He got off the bed and pulled the sheets and blankets over her and waited. He stayed in her room for three hours before going back to his own. She had gone to sleep almost as soon as he'd covered her up with the bedclothes.

He saw her three or four months later. He'd received a card telling him that some books he'd ordered had arrived and was on his way to collect them. It was one of those dark blue, blustery afternoons, late February, the sky too inky, the streets too dull for that hour. All day it had rained on and off. A warm, fresh, gusty wind, that seemed to be blowing directly off a high moor, billowed in the skirts of macintoshes and folded lapels against the wearers' cheeks. Yellow and pink neon, reflections from department store windows, streaked the wet pavings. He crossed the street, a café directly ahead of him, and saw her at one of the window tables. It was just her profile, but he knew who it was.

He walked to where the café's plate-glass window ended, and stopped so that he could look back. She wore a mottled, bottle-green velvet coat. The shoulder and upper sleeve on the left-hand side were pressed against the glass, showing a series of white-ish creases where the material was crushed. She was writing something. No one else was in there. She sat at her table by the window, leaning over a sheet of paper, writing. He inched forward and tried to read over her shoulder, but her arm and the faint glaze of condensation on the glass prevented him.

THE FOURTH YEAR

*

April

It was a sort of quieter Venice, so, in theory, it was a place they would like: at least, they agreed as much. They were looking for a restaurant, but didn't want to come upon it too soon – not before they'd walked up a few apparently unpromising alleys and made some discoveries. There would be some disappointments too, of course, but an hour of studiously pointless wandering would be bound to yield some sights. The trick was to get away from crowds and non-native tongues. In back-streets and tiny squares would be muttered conversation: casual exchanges at windows or on doorsteps – something said from a balcony, where washing was being collected, to someone invisible who sat beyond the shadow-line of full-length shutters. There would be children riding their bikes on the cobbles and scattering a flock of pigeons, small shops selling unrecognizable vegetables, televisions whitening walls. Their perfect eating place ought to be just on the edge of such a square – maybe a street away – and would elude them at first. They might mark it, wander on for a while, then backtrack; it would be what they often did.

The pigeons rose laconically and wheeled, finally descending all at once like a grey carpet on the farther side of the fountain, the rack and pinion of their wings squeaking as they back-pedalled for a landing. She had gone ahead – that was usual too. It was a tactic which prevented a too-precise sharing of memories. Her absences, whether they were for minutes or for days, often had to do with the fear of becoming part of a unit divisible by two – leaving nought. It chilled her to think of people who were never out of one another's company: all sights, all sounds, all events, oddities, little dramas, all people and places registering simultaneously and being for ever jointly owned. He'd remarked, once, that what she avoided didn't really exist: that the moment, the happening, even a view, couldn't strike them in just the same way. 'You precede me by a minute, let's say, into some street. Perhaps you suppose that by the time I arrive its aspect will have changed, even if only slightly. It will have been added to or subtracted from. But the addition and subtraction happens anyway; it has to do with how I see things, how you see them.'

'How much more irritating then,' she'd replied, 'to be asked "Do you remember?" '

She disappeared along a cul-de-sac that led to a church. He toured the square deferentially, looking into each window with a sly glance. Families were gathered at tables. During his first circuit he'd spotted a lively row: husband and wife yelling at each other from either end of the dinner-table, their children sitting mute between them. The hollow echoes of television sets and the rattle of radios on windowsills had covered the noise of the fight until he was close by the window. He approached for the second time and looked in. The bawling and tense gestures were finished. The man was standing at his wife's end of the table and gripping her by the forearm; the children were looking up. It was clear that something had just occurred in the room: everyone was motionless, occupying the pause that follows a fierce discharge of energy. As he watched, it began to peak once more. The woman's face had been turned; now she raised it and swore, but didn't try to tug her arm free. Her husband drew her towards him and slapped her again. Her head went sideways, though she wasn't riding the blow. She looked back at once and cursed him as she had before. The man switched his grip to her hair and shook her, yanking back and forth so that she almost toppled – would have, but for his support. She lashed out madly, never connecting, but her flying fists infuriated him and he hit her low to the stomach, pulling her on to the punch. She went down and out of sight; the man's arm was extended and he leaned forward slightly, still clutching his wife's hair.

There was a mass in progress. By the door was a basket of scarves and she'd draped one over her head like a mantle. She was at the very end of the nearest pew. He tiptoed across and for a while stood next to her as she knelt. He couldn't have sat down without disturbing her, so he went to the pew on the opposite side of the aisle and sat there. Close to the altar were twenty or so people, almost all women. The priest whispered through a microphone as he prepared the sacrament. Her stillness, he thought, was admirably maintained; it made speculation and desire rise in him like sap. He got up when she did and they walked to the door together after bending a knee reflexively. She appeared thoughtful, but he counted that for nothing; and, indeed, when they got outside she linked her arm with his and made him skip with her down the steps to the street.

They discovered a restaurant that was all they'd hoped for: and discovered it at just the time when they'd begun to want a drink. They ordered whisky, and then wine to go with a fish platter. She remarked on the fact that all European churches seemed to be enormous; he asked what she had prayed for. 'Oh, deliverance,' she said, grinning hugely. 'It's traditional.'

'From sin? From evil? From danger? From enemies? Friends?'

'Yes, all of that.'

'Which sins?'

'The lot; the lot. Deliverance from illness, too. And want. And hangovers.' She nudged her glass towards him and he filled it.

'God's bargain basement,' he observed. 'What would it be like, I wonder – deliverance from sin.'

'You'd tend to think of it more as something withheld, I imagine.'

'Depends on the sin.'

'Yes.'

'If sin it be.'

'It's clear to me that we're talking about lust.'

'Well, I thought you must be – given your judgement of my interpretation of deliverance.'

She topped and tailed a prawn and slapped it to and fro in a bowl of sauce. 'Somehow I don't think of you as one who would weigh the pros and cons of deliverance from greed or sloth.'

'Anger? Pride?'

'Just possibly. Not anger, I'd have thought?' She sucked the sauce off the prawn and dipped it again.

'No, you're wrong,' he said. 'I was considering the state of being recently delivered from sin, as if the soul had been given a going-over with a wire brush. Not a stain, not a blemish. How would you live in the world at all? Wouldn't you be like one of those people who suffer from total allergy and have to exist inside a plastic tent? You'd be too pure to touch anything.'

'Nonsense. You'd simply continue to be delivered. It would be like having total immunity, not allergy: as if you had just left the confessional but not yet emerged from the church.'

'That's just what I mean. You wouldn't want to sin – the desire would be a sin in itself. Delivered from that, you'd be too unsullied to exist. You'd vaporize – waft straight up, bathed in a golden glow, ringed by angelic choirs . . . or would you? I mean, no sin, no redemption.'

'You're saying I prayed for the impossible.'

'Well, no, I assume you meant deliverance on a piecemeal basis. Two Hail Marys and an Our Father – entirely possible, since that's the way it works. No, I was rather more thinking about what would happen if God took you at your word and permanently delivered you from sin. What form would a sinless being take? What's more, since it's inconceivable why are we held accountable for our sins?'

'Christ,' she said, 'we'll find you a Jesuit in the morning; ask him.'

He shared out the fish and refilled their glasses. 'No,' he said, 'I only just thought of that: the forgiveness of sin doesn't really come into it. I was proposing the notion of this sort of unbreathed-on creature . . . do you see?'

She said, 'Not really. You can be boring at times – do you know that?'

'What would you do,' he asked her, 'if I hit you – as hard as I could – in the stomach?'

She gave him a look of exasperation, then turned her head sideways to take a dripping prawn into her mouth. She spoke through the food. 'Am I expected to feel threatened?'

'No, of course not. It's a proposition that precedes a theory.'

'Is it? It sounded rather specific to me.'

'No, really.'

She pondered. 'Can't help you,' she said finally.

'Why not?'

'You wouldn't do such a thing.'

'I might . . . What do you mean, "wouldn't"?'

'If someone hurt me like that, I'd want revenge: want to return hurt for hurt. I know that; so do you. But you say if *you* hurt me in that way, so I have to think of you doing it. You wouldn't.'

'If I did, though . . .'

She laughed and picked up the carafe to pour some more wine. When their glasses were full, she reached over and gripped his hand, shaking it chidingly. 'Darling,' she said, still laughing, 'you simply wouldn't. Don't go *on* so. Drink your wine. Then let's go back. I'm tired; and I want us to look at the map.'

They decided to stay for at least three days since things had worked out so well. The weather was perfect. That morning they had stepped off the plane into searing sunlight: oven-like heat. The nights would be uncomfortable, perhaps, but they had already staked out a place for sunbathing – flat rocks and shoreline trees that always gave some shade – about four miles from the hotel. Three full days would establish her tan. They'd had luck with the hotel, managing to get a small suite in a dilapidated villa that stood well apart from the modern glass-and-steel building where most other people were staying. The villa had about twenty-five rooms but, it seemed, not more than half-a-dozen guests. They had a stone balcony almost directly above the sea, from which they could almost touch the uppermost part of one of the garden's cypresses. He opened the shutters on to its dark cone and a full moon directly ahead. 'We got sunlight on the sand,' he said, 'we got moonlight on the sea.'

She set the map aside and joined him on the balcony. From the terrace of the main building came the sound of an accordion and the drone singing makes when you're too far off to discern a tune. By leaning across their balustrade they could see lights among the trees and long tables covered by white cloths. Round two of the tables sat some thirty or forty forms swaying from side to side: four lines, each swaying in rhythmic opposition, and looking like some sort of perpetual motion machine. The musician walked round and between the tables in a slow, repetitive figure of eight. The song he played was unfamiliar, though it would dog them during the trip – be heard again and again on radios, on juke-boxes in cafés and over hotel Tannoy systems. They would find themselves whistling it, or humming it, and would laugh at first. Later, it would become as insistent and as involuntary as one of their own bad habits and cease to be a joke. The music and the voices swelled in unison as the catchy chorus was reached: the passage everyone knew.

'Do you suppose that will go on all night?' She lit a cigarette and retreated to the far end of the balcony, putting the terrace out of sight.

'Don't worry.' He disappeared for a minute, then returned with two glasses of pale brandy. 'I expect that in a short while they'll form ranks of three and march on Poland.'

They sat with their feet up on the stone railing, hearing the music and the sea, then, eventually, the sea alone. He finished his brandy and drank hers while she slept. She came to after he'd switched on one of the lamps and had begun to free the shutters. She stretched, making a little squeak, while he latched the bolts on one side, then glided through the half-shuttered space like someone who was last to leave a cinema or a darkening park, giving him a fuzzy smile as she passed.

*

They woke up to the sound of gunfire, a distant popping and crackling of carbines accompanied, sometimes, by the heavier, more even chug of something automatic. The car's engine masked it, but when they reached their spot for sunbathing they found they were closer to the noise and it took the edge off their pleasure. When he mentioned it she answered at once, as if she had been anticipating his question for so long that she'd become impatient to hear it and give her reply. 'A coup d'état,' she said, 'if you want my opinion. The borders will be closed. We'll be separated and sent to different camps where they specialize in torture techniques appropriate to either male or female physiology.' The sun was directly overhead; she slipped her T-shirt on. 'Pass me the water, will you?'

He shuffled over to her, holding the bottle and leering grotesquely. 'Perhaps I'll offer my services and claim you as my first victim.' While she drank, he walked his fingers upwards from her navel, *ho*, *ho*, *ho*-ing in a hollow voice. She turned his hand with the patient grace a mother will use to steer a child's sticky sweet away from her blouse – an accustomed, absent-minded gesture. She returned the bottle to him, shading her eyes to look round the small, almost circular bay. 'Is there anyone about?'

'Not that I can see.'

She hooked her bikini bottom down and kicked free of it, then picked her way over stones to the water some twenty feet away. She peed fastidiously into the sea's lip, scratching at some moss on a rock while she crouched. 'Shall we give it until three-thirty, then go back for a shower, perhaps?'

'Okay,' he said.

She clambered back to her rock and lay down as she was. 'Tell me if anyone comes.' She turned her face to the sun. Her aureoles showed as dark blots on the T-shirt. Last night, he recalled, she had worn a silk blouse that clung to the points of her breasts; had worn it open to the fourth button. Their waiter had lit her every cigarette. He was almost sure that when she clothed herself in that way it was without conscious intent.

Style, fashion, comfort even, were what dictated her choice and manner of wearing what she chose. She might become aware of the effect that she created, but that would be more likely to annoy than to please her – she seemed to count it a restriction on her freedom and claimed not to see the connection between dressing provocatively (fashionably, comfortably) and being desired. 'Are men really persuaded that easily?' she had once asked him. 'Will bits of women's bodies always do that?' There were times when he considered that she resembled nothing so much as a potential rape-victim with an innocent liking for dark alleys. He lay beside her and kept watch.

'Are you tired of the place?'

She had emerged from the shower and crossed the room to stand in a patch of sunlight, hanging her head to the right to towel her hair. Such moments always held his attention: when some small action would blanket thought. Her face was slack, her eyes fixed on the bars of sunlight drawn on one wall by the part-open shutters; her hands, meanwhile, worked briskly by her shoulder as she tossed the towel to find its drier parts, all the time flicking and patting her hair. When he spoke she threw her head back, then canted it to the left and began to dry from that side. 'Not at all,' she said. 'What made you think I might be?'

'We usually sunbathe for longer.'

'No, no. The freedom fighters in the hills were beginning to wear me down a bit.' She gave a last, vigorous, all-over rub before throwing the towel on to the bed. 'I've got a faint headache; it seemed like time to retreat. You didn't mind? I imagine it was the army's day for target practice.'

'Something of the sort. We could walk the walls, if you like.' He was lying on the bed, reading a guidebook he'd bought in London.

'We could?'

'You can walk right round, apparently.' He read from the book: ' "The old part of the city may be completely circumnavigated by walking along these fortifications." '

'Well, well. Yes, all right.' She dressed in two swift movements, then pushed her feet into sandals and walked to the door, opening it as if to usher him out. When he joined her she remained still for a second, one hand on the doorknob, and they stood in the doorway together. She chucked him under the chin and regarded him with a mock serious look. 'I love you,' she said.

To get to the old quarter it was necessary to cross a drawbridge. Just beyond it, they found the way on to the walls – a heavy, iron-bound door which opened on to an enclosed space the size of a large cupboard. Directly opposite, across six feet of stone floor, a wooden booth had been constructed inside a recess. An elderly man sat there; tickets and a cashbox lay on a narrow counter. The little cave was lit by an electric bulb above the custodian's head. A flight of stone stairs led off to one side.

When they came back into daylight after climbing only four steps of the first flight, they blinked and fumbled for sunglasses. Another three flights brought them to the top. The stone passage between the low crenellations was glassy with wear. On their right was the sea, empty and dizzying; the brilliant, unbroken blue of the sky seemed to drop below them on all sides.

'Will you be all right?'

'Sure.' She nodded, reaching down and out to lay her fingertips atop the parapet. 'Just take it slowly.'

'We could stop at the next lot of steps if you'd like.'

'Wherever they might be.'

'It's an astonishing view.'

'Lead on,' she said, looking fixedly at the back of his head. Then, almost at once, 'Not so quickly.'

As he walked, he looked inward – away from the harbour and the sea. The jumble of bright red roofs almost filled the circle, those in the middle distance and beyond appearing wholly undivided, like a canopy. It would have been easy to step down on to those that abutted the wall. It wasn't possible to see the centre – the cafés, the tourist shops. The narrow streets and tiny squares directly below were largely deserted. The wall was lower in some places than in others: sometimes he would find himself alongside the window to an upper room. On several occasions he stopped so abruptly that she almost walked into him and had to clutch at his arm to keep a balance. He saw an old woman in bed and, another time, someone closing a blind who looked back at him before shutting out the light.

It was worse when they met people coming from the opposite direction. In places where the wall dropped and the side of some building rose above it like a buttress she could move quickly to the house wall and put her shoulder blades to it, forcing others to pass her with only the crenellations for protection. Most often, though, it was a matter of choosing which side of the drop to come close to. Walking the narrow, polished pathway at all made her feel horribly precarious. She struggled to hold a straight line. It seemed that the space on either side tugged at her and she weaved a little as she walked, as if constantly counteracting a pull from the left, then from the right. She felt on the very top of things, stranded in blue, likely to pitch over into the void at any time.

'I didn't know it would be this bad,' he called over his shoulder. His capable tone made her grit her teeth. This might be retaliation for – what? His nervousness about the gunfire? For disappearing into the church while out of his sight? He was varying his pace – sometimes walking on just a shade too briskly, then slowing as if suddenly recalling her fear. Because she needed to be close to him, she found herself trotting and stopping, trotting and stopping, like a child who can't properly match its parents' stride. After fifteen minutes she was washed out and trembling, not able to slacken concentration in order to find a cigarette, not able to call a halt, since there was only the path, the knee-high crenellations, and the sky. Twice they had to stand aside while others overtook them and she felt the awful vacancy at her back, its magnetism.

Half-way round she discovered an escape route – a long

stairway that led directly into a back-street. 'You don't have to,' she told him. 'Why don't you go the rest of the way?' But then, after she'd walked down no more than a dozen steps, she froze, clutching the rope that was tacked to the wall and shrinking from the sheerness on her other hand. She had once seen a staircase in a partly demolished house fixed, like this, on only one side and descending through air. Just to look had made her sway. Eventually he climbed down ahead of her and faced backwards, taking first one ankle and then the next to guide her feet on to each new step. At the bottom she cried, sitting on the lowest step with her head in her hands. He sat beside her, his arm round her shoulders. As she began to speak the wife-beater passed them, pushing a bicycle. The man had only been seen through a window for a minute, but his moustache and his thin face were immediately recognizable.

She was wiping her nose and looking at him for a response. 'You want to go back?' He thought that was what she'd said.

'I really have got an awful headache. I'd just like to lie down with the shutters drawn and be quiet.'

'Fine,' he said, 'I'll wander about some more.'

She looked at her watch. 'Can you stay out till six? I'll probably sleep.'

'Okay – six.'

She hesitated, wondering whether he might be going to walk part-way to the drawbridge with her, but he grinned and raised a hand and backed off a couple of paces. When she looked back from the corner it was with the genuine intention of giving him a smile and a wave; she was surprised to find no one there, and was not pleased.

The square was no more than a couple of streets away. The husband had leant his bike against the fountain and was sitting outside his front door, drinking wine with a friend; apart from the three of them, the square was empty. Almost opposite the house was a small bar. He sat there in the shade of the one umbrella. No one came out to sell him a drink. He waited; and in a short while the wife appeared with a shopping basket and spoke to her husband who nodded, then, all of a sudden, laughed and batted her on the backside. She grinned and swung the basket at his head.

When she left he followed. The husband shouted something and laughed again, but she didn't turn. They ambled towards the busier part of the town: she was in no hurry and he had to judge his pace carefully in order to not go too close. Light-brown hair, he noted, quite pretty – attractive at any rate – and slim, but nonetheless rounded in the way that southern women often are. Her breasts, he remembered, were round, not gravid or sharp, and her buttocks were round; the light, flower-patterned cotton of her frock clung to them, wrinkling slightly, and he could discern a little tremble beneath the material when they tightened and dropped as she walked. She was twenty-eight he decided. There was something faintly sluttish about the way she carried herself, something that came of the heat, of being poor and complaisant. He imagined how she would put a dress on over her slip only in order to go out of doors.

He stood near her as she began to select vegetables and fruit from racks outside a shop, then moved to be alongside and reached across to take a melon from the display, making sure that their hands collided. They apologized in their respective languages and their hands drew back. Knowing that she wouldn't understand him, he was tempted to speak: 'I've followed you from your house', or 'I know that your husband beats you'. He didn't of course; but the impulse preoccupied him and, for a few seconds, he stared at her. The smile with which she had accepted his apology slackened, though she was embarrassed and tried to maintain it. When he didn't move she stuttered some words; then, shielded by his inability to know what she'd said, picked up the melon and handed it to him, nodding and smiling firmly once more. 'Oh, yes,' he nodded too, as if in affirmation, 'thank you,' and went into the shop to pay.

Their room was sunlit and empty. He found her, after checking the pool-side, in the bar of the main hotel, an untouched beer in front of her and the map spread across her lap. The headache had gone almost at once she told him, so she'd decided to go for a walk.

'You didn't sleep?'

'I lay down for ten minutes and felt fine.'

'You looked really quite ropy when you left me.'

'I wasn't in great shape; it didn't persist, thank God.'

'Where did you go?'

'I walked back into the town and wandered for a bit. Had a coffee. There was a recital in one of the churches.'

'A what?'

'A recital. You know: concert. It was free. I walked past the door and heard the music. I stayed until it was over. What about you?'

'The same, really. Didn't come across any free concerts. I bought us a melon for when we're sunbathing tomorrow, then just pottered to and fro.'

'Look,' she said, 'how do you feel about maybe moving on tomorrow?'

'The villa's very nice.'

'I know.' She shrugged.

'Yes, okay,' he said. Then, when she went back to the map, 'Do you want that beer?'

When they went out the Germans were assembling at the tables on the terrace, greeting friends with shouts of laughter, each couple making directly for this or that certain pair of seats. 'They have set places – the same chair each night,' she said. 'How odd.' Walking towards the town they elaborated on the theme, inventing tortuous compulsion-neuroses. It was a way of reassuring one another about their own mildly eccentric method of travelling. In truth he would have liked to stay another full day but he trusted her instinct: she usually led in such matters and, most often, something happened to prove that her judgements were better than his. Staying too long, she had observed, was like over-eating; she managed to organize things so that they left with the entirely pleasant feeling that they could have taken just a little more. Because he'd made the concession, however, he would probably be able to choose where they would eat and began to steer her towards the restaurant they'd been to on the previous night.

'Do you really want to?' He knew from her tone that she didn't much mind. Even so, he presented his case: 'It was the only reasonable one we found that wasn't near the main square. The menu was good. We'd probably wind up going there anyway.'

Since he was leading she hung back a little, pausing to look at the goods in tiny shops, trying to decipher the gist of some poster, now and then taking a few steps along a side-street, perhaps in the hope of happening upon a different, more interesting eating-place. When he reached the square she was some way behind. The husband's bicycle was still leaning against the fountain. A light was on in the downstairs room. He went at once to the window intending, if he saw nothing, to pass it, then turn and look in from the other angle; but as he drew level, the woman – who must have been approaching the window from inside the room as he approached it from the street – appeared there, her hand on the lower sash as if she were about to open it. The encounter was too sudden to permit either of them the chance of looking away. A fraction of a second's difference and an acknowledging stare might have become a glance; as it was, they met head-on. His chin rose slightly, assertively, probably because there was no way to dissemble. When she moved out of sight he retreated to the far side of the square.

The door opened and the husband stepped outside, then advanced a few paces shouting and waving an arm. His wife stood in the doorway. The shouts echoed in the silent square and other people came to their doors. 'What's going on?' She walked to join him, looking, all the time, at the husband who had come as far as the fountain and was standing by it, hands on hips, as if it represented a frontier. 'It doesn't matter.' He put an arm round her shoulders and kissed her firmly. When he saw

88

this, the husband's unintelligible questions stopped; he turned and looked at his wife.

'Come on.' They walked out of the square, he with his arm still slung across her shoulders, keeping their pace steady until they were clear. A street away, he put his hands into his pockets and lengthened his stride a little.

'What was all that about?'

'Not sure. I was waiting for you. Perhaps I looked suspicious: a loiterer brimming with intent.'

'He just appeared and started yelling?'

'I was ambling round the square. Yes.'

'You'd think they'd be used to sightseers.'

'Or fed up with them perhaps. Who knows?'

They found the restaurant and were given the table they'd had before. The waiter smiled broadly at her when he returned with the wine and said something to her that neither could quite catch. She had been puzzled by the incident, then had become indignant, then curious. 'Were you frightened?'

He drank some wine. 'I was a bit. People had begun to appear at their doors.'

'Perhaps they'd had some burglaries, or muggings.'

'Yes, could be. That might well be it.'

'You should have said something – to show that you're foreign.'

'I suppose so. It didn't occur to me.' They looked at their menus and sat in silence for a while until she managed to make the waiter see her half-raised hand. 'Though what would I have said?'

'Doesn't matter. Anything. "My postilion has been struck by lightning." Anything.' He began to chuckle, his glass at his lips, then had to put it down as the laugh took hold of him. 'What?' she asked.

'I was imagining a bilingual version. The guy yelling, "What are you hanging round for? Are you a mugger? What's your game? Piss off, or I'll call the police," while I'm shrieking "My postilion has been struck by lightning." If there happened to be someone around who spoke both languages, I'd probably have wound up in the state nuthouse.' He picked up his glass again, but now he'd started laughing he was finding it difficult to stop. She looked on, grinning, until his giggles petered out.

They agreed that the meal was good: that they had been right to return to that restaurant. She took out a cigarette and the waiter came over to light it. Then she unfolded the map, turning it towards him so that he could help to select a route.

THE FOURTH YEAR

*

September

'It's a man who is too badly wounded to move. The battle-axe that has almost severed his arm is still wedged fast between the armour's plating where his adversary slammed it. He suspects that he is going to die, although he hasn't yet fully admitted it, so he's not resigned to the notion; which, possibly, is why he's still alive. The noise around him, of men crying or lowing with pain, seems to coalesce in a single, deep ululation: rising, abating, rising again. If he lifts his head he can see the broken ground of the battlefield and the strewn forms of the dying – hundreds of them; but it hurts him to do this and, in any case, he doesn't want to look. He's already assured himself that none of the enemy troops are walking the field to dispatch the wounded and that the looters have not yet arrived. For most of the time he looks at the sky and the circling crows. Now and then something rustles nearby or scuttles over his legs. There are no trumpets, no sounds of horses; there's no bellowing, no rattle of weapons. The air is still. It's early, but already a haze hangs like a distant curtain on all sides. The other sound, echoing the first, is the unremitting drone of flies. His mouth is so dry that it feels as though it were lined with salt. Something has caked in his throat. He thinks that if a wind were to get up, a wind from the west, it would bring rain: not a downpour but a light, persistent fall to dissolve the parch in his mouth runnel by runnel, trickling into his gullet and clearing it. He lies there, his legs, in their chain-mail, stretched out like an effigy's, near dead from blood-loss, the pain so constant that he almost no longer resents it, and wishes for the rain. Then, having dreamed of the almost possible, thinks another, impossible, thought. That's one interpretation; anyway, it's the one I like best.'

93

'It makes a good story,' she said. Then: 'Say it again.'

'Western wind, when wilt thou blow, The small rain down can rain, Christ, if my love were in my arms, And I in my bed again.' Because he'd already spoken the lines, he delivered them conversationally – a recapitulation.

She pondered. 'I'm not convinced that if I were in his predicament I'd be likely to invent an erotic fantasy.'

'I don't think that's quite what he's supposed to have in mind.'

'I was *teasing*.' She chuckled at the predictable irritation in his voice, kicking his foot under the covers, then shrugged more securely into the crook of his arm. He moved his hand from where it lay, lightly, across her ribs, to cup her mound. Obediently, she opened her legs. After a minute or two she slid deeper into the bed, cooing, and reached down to better position his finger. She looked docile. She smiled and closed her eyes. He didn't see her open them again that night.

When he'd switched off the lamp, she turned and nestled her backside against his stickiness, then hauled his arm over her body, twining her fingers with his. He could feel her breath on the back of his hand. She kissed his knuckles and offered a long hum of approval. 'Sometimes,' she said, 'it's like eating chocolate soufflé.'

James was drunk; he'd been drunk when he arrived. Anna, seated on the opposite side of the dinner table, glanced at him continually – sometimes issuing a warning, sometimes simply looking concerned. She couldn't manage to catch his attention: he was too animated. She closed her eyes as someone fielded a dish that was wobbling wildly in her husband's grip. He missed completely with a potato which bumped from the rim of his plate on to the table and then on to the floor and out of sight, but James didn't see it and nor did anyone else. From time to time Anna lifted the pelmet of tablecloth from her lap and looked among the shifting feet, trying to locate it. Maybe she could hook it towards her before it was crushed, slippery with butter, into the carpet. She had a vision of the dinner-party repairing to the drawing-room and someone pausing to lift a shoe, as people do when they suspect they've trodden in dog shit, and finding the greasy pat fixed there and a track leading away from the table.

She winced as James helped himself to wine and then made two attempts to get the bottle back into the coaster before Tim guided it into place with a discreet fingertip. There was, she felt, some distaste about the discretion. James ate with a whisky-hunger, letting a French bean slip from his mouth as he spoke. 'Ours are at the mucky stage. Mark's got a pile of glossies under his bed, split-beaver shots all coated with lashings of lubricant.' He emphasized the first syllable, mooing it: 'loobricant'; a gloating lasciviousness. His shoulders heaved as he laughed. 'All these bloody wenches in garter-belts, socking great tits sellotaped to attention, with their fingers on – what's the plural of clitoris? Have you ever wondered who takes the pictures? I mean, it's a bloody odd sort of a line, isn't it? Can you imagine someone stocking his gadget-bag before setting off to the studio? "Lenses – yes, filters – yes, KY – yes . . ." There was one shot of this big blonde in transparent knickers, bending over to show you her bum. I mean, nothing changes, does it? We used to do that as kids: "Show us your bum for a boiled sweet" sort of thing. He keeps them under the bed. Sarah's the same. Anna found all these dirty stories in her dressing-table drawer, didn't you? All handwritten. Obviously, they circulate at her school. What I want to know is, who makes them up? They were all black along the folds, like some letter you've had in your wallet for years. Someone must. It's like jokes.'

Erica smiled a thank-you and took the bowl of peas from Anna. She put half a tablespoonful on to her plate and passed the bowl on. 'They don't have to be funny,' said James, 'as long as they're to do with sex. When they're seven or eight, it's all lavatories and farting. Then it's rubbers and so forth. All that slang – it's sort of coy, I suppose. We used to call sanitary towels "jam-rags". "What's the worst sign of poverty? A jam-rag with a laundry mark." Used to crease us up, that sort of thing.'

Erica accepted some more wine. To Anna, she said, 'Tim took Henry to watch their team play last Saturday. Outside the ground there were these National Front people dishing out leaflets. Apparently they're on duty every time there's a match.'

'Two men in camelhair coats,' Tim said, 'about twenty bald teenage thugs wearing Doc Martens, and two little old women, for Christ's sake.'

Erica nodded. 'One of the boys had a swastika tattooed on his forehead. They wear Union Jack T-shirts and studded leather wristbands. You daren't say anything.'

'The Tory Party in battledress,' Tim observed.

'And the police just mill around, you know, searching the occasional kid going in to the match. Nothing's said.'

Tim was leaning on the table with both forearms, hunched over eagerly, his head ducking and thrusting, impatient to re-enter the conversation, like a child whose turn it is to skip anticipating the flight of the rope.

'Did you say anything?' asked Anna.

'Are you serious? I had Henry with me for one thing. Who can say anything to them? Look at the way the media panders to youth: fashions, cults, their Christ-awful music; it's all taken so seriously. Capitalism knows when it's on to a good thing. Cannon-fodder or an inexhaustible source of revenue – it's all the same. And the mindless buggers do just what's required of them: die or spend. If someone tells them to hate niggers and Jews, they'll do that too. Or hero-worship some brain-damaged multi-millionaire guitarist.'

'You know the famous London hum?' James asked. Erica shook her head. 'Sometimes at night there's a hum – seems to come from just outside, except it seems that way to everyone who hears it. No one knows what it is. There was a series of articles in the press about it; people were being driven barmy; entire districts of the city plagued by insomnia. You must have heard it: sounds like the whine of a generator; irritating monotone.'

'No,' said Erica.

'You've heard it, haven't you darling?' Anna nodded without looking up from her food. A new bottle of wine was brought to the table and James pushed his glass forward as he spoke. 'Well, my theory is that in our area there are so many feminists, lesbians and ill-served wives that what the insomniacs of North One can hear is the drone of ten thousand vibrators being wielded in unison. The massed dildoes of Islington Green.'

Tim aligned his knife and fork on his empty plate. 'I haven't heard it,' he said, 'but then Erica and I sleep like the dead.'

'Henry gets up and makes his own breakfast at weekends, now,' said Erica, 'and he's got a TV in his room. My only problem is getting the peanut-butter off his pillowslips.'

'It's okay.' Anna paused, smiling, and placed a hand over her glass, refusing the pudding wine. 'In fact, it's more than okay. I'm really enjoying it. The only bugbear is that I have to share an office. It means more travelling, of course. That doesn't please James.' Her husband's head was drooping over his plate and swaying slightly from side to side in an oddly bovine motion. He lifted his eyes when he heard his name mentioned, but hadn't caught the sense of what had been said. He smiled a tame, wet smile and nodded as if in agreement.

'What about the kids?' Erica asked.

'There's the au pair –'

'Of course, yes, you told me. Is she capable?'

'Oh, yes.'

'Some flaxen-haired Brunnhilde?' Tim suggested. He cupped his glass and swilled the wine like brandy, hoping the gesture wouldn't be missed. 'She must have a lively time with James and Mark around the place.'

'She's Italian,' Anna said and got up to help carry the dishes to the sink.

On his way back from the kitchen, he collected the brandy and a box of cigars. It might, he thought, be necessary to feed the liquor to James with the aid of a spoon. From where he sat, he could see her through the kitchen door, chatting to Anna as she made the coffee. She laughed and shook her head and put out a sympathetic hand – Anna had made an extravagant gesture that involved thrusting her fingers into her hair and tugging at her own head like a hysteric.

Where had it been? Tim and Erica, James and Anna, one or two others . . . Somewhere out of doors, a summer, maybe a couple of years ago. A place in the country; but it had been near London and there was water. A regatta . . .? Rain had threatened, then the weather had become bright and blowy. They had been very taken up with one another: happy to join in whatever it had been that the day involved; but smiling and touching. Swans, he thought, there had been swans. Maidenhead, perhaps? There had been lots of people: a throng.

She had worn a light macintosh over a print skirt and a high-necked blouse. There had certainly been some spectacle, because they'd stood to watch and then, a little later, had leaned against railings above the water, he with his back to them, she leaning lightly against him, her hands on the railings so that their stomachs touched. His arms had encircled her, his fingers laced casually on the small of her back, as they both looked sideways at – what? – oarsmen? A few seconds later she had moved closer to let a stream of people pass by, and dabbed him with a kiss. He'd grinned, slipping his hands inside her mac to join them again low on her hips, then had found the zip at the back of her skirt and, after a moment's hesitation, had unfastened it, pushing under her knickers to cup a buttock in either hand. Her lips had pursed in mock outrage. They'd stood for a moment or two, shifting their feet as a gathering queue edged past, making for . . . a pub? An exit? Then he'd eased one of her cheeks sideways and plugged the little finger of the other hand an inch or so into her arse. Her eyes had widened and she'd yelled with laughter – a whooping, involuntary laugh that began with two or three plosive sounds in her chest and emerged as an ill-disguised bray; a noise that betrayed shock almost instantly becoming glee. All the while she had been looking away from him towards a curtain of willow and a boathouse by a bend in the river.

She came in with the coffee tray and a plate of petits fours. Setting the tray down on the table, she took from him the cheese and the butter dish he'd lifted to make room. 'Butter,' she said, 'in a lordly dish.' He listened for a trace of combativeness in her tone, but there was none.

'*She* was Italian,' announced Tim. He had directed the remark to Erica who took the cup that was being proffered and looked across the table with raised eyebrows.

'Who?'

'The girl in that newspaper story.'

'Ah, yes; the cupboard.'

Tim guffawed. 'There was a piece in the paper last week about some girl – I'm sure she was Italian; it wasn't in Italy though – who'd had a baby, or was pregnant – wasn't that it –?'

'Pregnant,' Erica said.

'– Who locked her boyfriend, the father, in a cupboard when he said he was going to leave her – and kept him there. I mean, he *died.*'

'You mean she just went away?' Anna asked. 'Leaving him in the –'

'No. Christ, no. She was in the house, flat, whatever, all the time. I mean, this guy was yelling and pounding and pleading to be let out, or so I imagine; anyway – promising to stand by her, I expect, and swearing undying fealty; she just left him there. Wouldn't have it. Didn't believe him, I suppose. I don't know.'

James had revived a little with the brandy. 'Why didn't he kick it down? Silly sod.'

'Thick door, small cupboard, I imagine,' replied Tim. 'Doors don't invariably reduce to matchwood if kicked like in the movies, you know.' He pointed to the dining-room door. 'Could you smash your way through that if it was trapping you inside a space just big enough to hold a few clothes?'

'What happened?'

Tim turned back to Anna. 'He died. Starved to death, it seems. She just kept him in there until he died. How many days would that be?'

'It's water, isn't it?' said Erica. 'He'd die of thirst really; the hunger would be a secondary thing. How long do those hunger-strikers last?'

'Two weeks, is it?' James sipped his brandy; at once he appeared very drunk again. His speech took on the careful, orotund, almost inchoate throatiness of someone who is aware of his drunkenness but too far gone to either enunciate clearly or shut up altogether. His left eye was watering. 'Maybe longer. Three weeks. Last one.'

Erica laughed. 'God, I hadn't thought of it like that. Three weeks of days and nights and this poor sod bashing on the door.'

Anna flapped a hand for attention. 'Wait a minute, I'm not sure I've got this entirely. She did it because –'

'She was pregnant by him,' Erica interrupted.

'And he said he wasn't going to stick around.' Tim shrugged. 'That's all it was.' He said: 'Must have been love.'

'Or desperation,' observed Anna.

James fumbled his glass. 'I'd've been bloody desperate. Some cow locked me in a cupboard three weeks. Fuck me.' He started to laugh and soon was roaring uncontrollably, slapping the table, rocking his chair back on two legs. He paused, hooting, to wipe his eyes with the heel of one hand. 'Oh, Christ,' he said. 'Fuck me.' Then went back to shouting with laughter until Anna couldn't help but join in. She'd never been able to resist his laugh.

*

They were the last to go. As they stood on the threshold, James tried to prise the car keys from Anna's grip. His foot slipped off the edge of a step and he clutched the doorframe. 'Come on,' he said. 'Hasn't been a jam-jar built I can't drive.' Again his foot missed a step and his momentum carried him, stumbling, on to the pavement. He lost his bearings for a second or two, then turned, reaching up to paw Anna's arm. 'Hasn't been a jam-jar built I can't drive.'

Anna smiled and went down to the car. She waved as she unlocked the door and climbed in. James stood on the other side waiting to be admitted, his arm along the car's roof, his head on his arm. The door opened and struck him, but he didn't move until Anna blew the horn; then he came to, pulled at the door, and fell inside. It was a full minute before the door closed and the engine started.

'James was in a bad way.'

'James was in a bad way,' he agreed and squeezed some washing-up fluid into the bowl. 'Where was it we went with them? Tim and Erica were there too, having a tiff over something.'

'I don't know. Where?'

'Summer, two – three years ago. By the river. I don't really remember the occasion: what was going on, or why we all went.'

'I don't know,' she said. Then, 'Cookham.'

'Cookham. Yes.'

'Yes,' she smiled. 'I remember. Do you want some music on while we do this?'

'Not particularly.' His shoulders fell and he stopped sponging the plates for a moment, but dabbled his hands idly among the suds. 'Why do we see them?'

She laughed. 'Christ alone knows. We have them together – that's the only virtue.'

'It's bloody depressing.'

'Yes, it is.' She nudged him and he went back to the plates, scratching at some encrustation with a thumb-nail. 'Tim's cupboard story was odd.'

'I saw it. Can't remember which paper. Very odd, yes. I thought the girl was Italian, too; or maybe Spanish.' He had tried to imagine the progression. What had the girl said? 'Could you fetch my coat from the cupboard?' Perhaps they had been going out: the man for the last time, knowing that it wasn't quite over yet but wanting to be out, outside, somewhere on what he thought of as neutral ground. The house – the flat? – would have seemed a trap, his back to each of the walls at one time or another during the month – week? day? – when they had both known what he intended. To get outside: that would have seemed the first step, even if it meant that the girl must come too. And perhaps she would see, once they were out, that it was possible. The flat had about it too much of their shared life. What bonded them was the mirror they had bought in a New Year's sale, the vase they always moved from the table when friends came to dinner, the dishes on display, the books they had brought back from holiday, their pages gummed with sun-tan oil, the cat that was now two years old (he had fixed a spare length of carpeting to half-way up the wall in one corner of the room so that it could claw there), the scarf he had chosen for her last birthday. 'Could you fetch my scarf from the cupboard?' And then he hadn't left: there was the door, unopened. Once that was true, once that much was true, what else was there to do? What else was there that she could have said? Or had it been anger? Was it possible, perhaps, that finally she had become angry?

No. No, but he would have been angry – the man; though maybe not at first. In the dark, he might have closed his eyes and let out his breath in an aggrieved sigh, thinking: *Bitch; stupid bitch*, and have realized that the sedate end of things that he'd planned (he might even have allowed himself 'poignant') was a forlorn hope. Before he began spasmodically to thump on the thick panels of the door, before he began to yell and curse her, before he lost his temper or, later, felt a nip of fear and started thinking of how he might prise out the hinge bolts with a wire coat-hanger, long before he realized it was an outwards-opening door as all cupboard doors are, he would probably have said, quite casually, something like: 'Don't be foolish, Maria. Come on. Open the door. It's no good.'

'Her name was Maria something.'

'So she could have been either – Italian, or Spanish.'

'I guess so.' He set two wine glasses down on the draining-board and she picked one up to dry it. 'It is odd. I mean, she'd have known, each day, that he was behind the door, dying. She'd hear him – have to listen to him. I wonder what she did.'

'How do you mean?'

'Well, I wonder: did she cook meals for herself, watch TV, read books? Did she go out shopping from time to time and come back to him – still in there; and if she did might she, without thinking, have called out "It's me, I'm back", or whatever? Did she occasionally put her hand out to the cupboard's door-handle when she'd taken her coat off, forgetting he was in there? I mean, how did she occupy herself? Did she hoover and put the washing-machine on and feed the cat?'

'Was there a cat?'

'I'm speculating. Take the cat as read.'

'Okay,' she chuckled. 'Maybe she bombarded him with homilies. You know –' She cupped her hands round her mouth and raised the pitch of her voice to convey something shouted – 'Least said soonest mended, Luigi. You've made your bed and you lie on it. Or, your chickens have come home to roost, you bastard.'

'He wasn't Italian – she was.'

'Oh, okay; not Luigi – Darrell.'

'Darrell?'

'I sort of had him as a semi-skilled type.'

'You're a snob, you know.' He kept back the last brandy glass and rinsed the suds off under the tap before going to the drinks tray and pouring himself a dribble. 'Let's do the pans tomorrow. I don't see him at all like that.'

She took the glass away from him, sipped, and gave it back. 'And her?'

'No clear picture. But I want to know what she *did*. He must have pleaded with her for hours – I mean days.'

She was folding the tablecloth and stopped to drum her fists on the edge of the table. 'Let me out. Let me out, let me out, let me out, you stupid bitch.'

He put his fingers in his ears and turned his head away from her, coquettishly. In a sing-song voice, she called: 'You can't keep me in here for ev–er.' He looked towards her, his hand to his mouth, as if suddenly struck by an idea.

'Let me out you cow, or I'll break your back.'

His eyebrows lifted. He said, 'Her eyebrows lifted and a tiny smile played about her lips.'

She sat down and panted, stretching her arms before her and to the side, miming claustrophobia. Putting a stutter of apprehension in her tone, she said: 'Maria. It's okay, Maria. I'll stay. I'll stay with you and be a father to the bambino.'

He leapt to his feet and made the motions of someone hoovering.

'I promise, Maria. Cross my heart and hope to die.'

He drowned her out with an extravagantly loud droning.

'Maria – we could take a holiday. Would you like that? We could go back to the Adirondacks.'

He droned louder and an octave higher, then stopped abruptly. 'Adirondacks?'

She dropped the imploring tone. 'Oh, well – Benidorm, then; who's the snob now? Come on Maria,' she took up the role again, 'I didn't mean what I said. I know it's mine.'

He put the hoover away and opened an invisible tin. Then he poured milk into a saucer. 'Puss,' he trilled, 'puss, puss, puss. Come on, pussy-puss.'

She slid to the floor, sitting with her head bowed, her hands folded limply in her lap. 'I'm thirsty. I'm thirsty and hungry. Do you want me to die in here?'

He put the food and milk down on the floor. 'There we are, puss. My, you were ready for that, weren't you?'

Her voice deepened to a narrator's monotone. 'The hours became days; the days became a week. Trapped behind the stout oak of the cupboard door, Darrell grew weaker . . . weaker and more terrified. Slowly, but with awful inevitability, the terrible ordeal began to unhinge his mind.' She whipped her fingers through her short hair, causing it to stand up in tufts. 'Maria,' she croaked. 'Maria. I want to come out, Maria.' Her fingernails raked the carpet, making tearing sounds. 'I want to come out, Maria. We can be together for ever, Maria. Come in here with me. It's safe and warm in here. Bring the baby in, Maria.'

He sniffed convulsively, wiping imaginary tears from his cheeks, but turned his back and shook his head. She ran out of inventions and lay on the floor, still raking the carpet, emitting little gagging noises that were Darrell's death-rattle. Then she rolled over on to her back, knees and elbows bent, unblinking eyes staring straight up at the ceiling.

He swallowed his brandy and walked into the kitchen to sluice the glass. He heard her giggle, then cough – a little spate of coughing brought on by the death throes. He went back to find her full-length on the carpet, fingers laced behind her head to prop it up.

'What do you suppose he did about – as it were – the lavatory?'

'Yes,' he said, 'I hadn't thought of that.'

Near dawn they both woke up and he fetched tea while she dried her face and went to the bathroom. He could hear her rattling bottles in the medicine cabinet. She returned wearing her bathrobe and blowing her nose in a series of loud, practical honkings, pressing first one nostril, then the other, and finally scrubbing the tissue across the septum in a businesslike, no-nonsense manner.

'It was so silly,' she said, 'so obvious.' She laughed, getting back into bed without removing the towelling robe. Taking the cup he'd placed on the bedside table, she sipped and shivered. 'It's cold, isn't it?'

'The cupboard,' he stated.

'Oh, yes: silly. That and the story you made up about the wounded knight. When was it? A week ago?'

'Longer than that.' He gave her a pointed look, but thought better of it and cocked an eyebrow and smiled with one corner of his mouth in order to make it seem no more than a passing remark. She put her cup down a trifle too heavily and he ran the conversation on. 'I didn't make it up exactly. What happened?'

'There's a lot I can't get back.' She frowned. 'It was my parents' house: in the spare bedroom, I think. But I can't recall what else happened. Something was going on in the garden . . . yes, a big party; a garden-party. I don't know. Some of my schoolfriends were there – I mean, we were children. Then I was in the bedroom; in fact I was getting out of the bed; and when I opened the cupboard door it was like one of those fairy stories when a kid discovers a new land behind a door or a curtain. Inside the cupboard was the field – it was an outdoors scene. I was in the bedroom, looking through the open door at the field and the sky and trees in the distance . . . distant hills and so forth. And at first the man was right at my feet – sometimes he was. At other times he was mixed up with piles of others in the middle distance. The garden-party . . . ?' She frowned again. 'He sort of came and went. At one time, I think, the cupboard was full of rats, running over him. It wasn't the field that time. But mostly it was and he was close enough to me so that I could see him clearly – just underfoot. His arm had come off and the stump was gushing, like one of those yard pumps where the water comes in a great gout every time you lever down, then stops when you lever up. I had the feeling that I was . . . like one of those women who used to watch cavalry charges in the Crimea or wherever it was. You know – little camp stools, a vantage point, a cold collation and an officer to explain the finer points of either side's tactics. I mean, it wasn't odd that I should be there, but somehow I was too close. I could smell everything;

I was closer than was proper; and I was on my own. I'm sorry.'
She lifted her cup. 'It's not fair. I never listen to yours.'

He shook his head. 'It's okay. I'm awake. Who was the man
– knight?'

'Mmmm . . .' She pondered a moment. 'Don't know. No one.
I mean, just a man.'

'Darrell?'

'Could be.'

'Tim?' he went on. 'Me? James?'

'No,' she said, 'I don't think so. No.'

'What woke you up?'

She answered at once. 'Oh, I think it was the blood. It got on
me. There were lots of other parts – sort of disconnected. It
didn't all happen in order. You know: dreams. You think that if
you concentrate it'll all come back – a narrative. But they're not
like that. There were other bits.' Her eyes closed briefly; she
opened them to smile. 'I'm sorry I've made you wakeful.'

'Don't worry.'

She loosened the belt of her robe but kept it on, lifting the
collar as if against a draught. Her eyelids rose and fell, then
again, then again, a tiny morse for sleep, each time staying
closed a little longer. 'I've taken a pill.'

'Sure,' he said, 'okay.' He put his cup down and she stretched
out an arm, covering his hand with her own. He took it, at first,
to be a mild gesture of gratitude, a small thing, a token between
people familiar with one another; not something you would
remember; done almost by reflex. But she opened her eyes once
more and smiled again and squeezed his fingers before the light
went out; and as he put his head on the pillow he wondered
whether he'd caught, in the smile, a startled pity that he hadn't
troubled to look for earlier.

THE FIFTH YEAR

*

February

He began at the nick of the doe's cunt. Using the tip of the knife he made two quick incisions, then a long cut up to the throat. He put the knife down and yanked the skin back, easing the hind- and fore-paws out as if he were undressing an infant. He turned the creature over and peeled the skin off its back, pulling upwards towards the head. It came free with a neat ripping sound. He took a cleaver and severed the head. The flayed torso lay on the chopping-board; the rag of the pelt hung down like a mummer's disguise from the still-fleshed head. He set it aside and started again with the knife, opening the paunch, using the same upward cut. The guts slipped out in a quick tangle. The dog lay with haunches cantilevered, her fore-legs stretched straight ahead, watching him. She had caught the rabbit an hour or so earlier on the high field west of the house. He had restrained her with the slip-leash, circling to stay downwind, until they were close enough for the chase to be pretty much even odds: the rabbit was feeding close to gorse where the burrows would be. She'd walked alongside, tense, eyes fixed on her prey, her long ears standing straight and fluttering minutely like ash leaves. He loved to watch her when she came alert: scenting or seeing a quarry. Most often she would walk with her head on a plane with her backbone, ears laid flat and pointing back. When she started to hunt the ears would rise, the neck become almost vertical; and she'd seem to walk on tiptoe, the big muscles in her hind legs growing taut, the hide contracting across her rib-cage. It was as if her components, loosely connected, suddenly assembled along the line of herself. Her narrow, bevelled head would snap round to observe any movement on the landscape.

He had stopped and put his thumb to the leash's trigger

release, feeling her pull slightly against the check. Then he'd pressed and the collar had fallen open and she'd gone: into her full stride at once, it seemed, from a standing start. Her speed, and the explosion of action as she left his side, was shocking – exhilarating. She'd run the rabbit down somewhere amid the gorse and emerged with it as he galloped up the slope, labouring in his wellingtons. 'Good girl,' he'd said, 'good girl,' extending one hand for the rabbit, the other to rest on her shoulder. She had growled as he'd taken the creature from her – a deep rumble from the sharp, bowed prow of her chest – but had let it go. He'd killed it with a chop to the back of the neck and thrust it into his bag.

It was a cool morning of brilliant blue. As they had approached the high field, he'd noticed that the valley was filled with songbirds. On one side a bank of trees ascended two hundred feet – solid foliage. A heron had risen from the stream that creased the valley floor, and for a full ten minutes he'd been able to watch the pair of buzzards that owned the canopy of sky between the hills, floating along one crest until the escarpment's thermal hit them and they rose, spiralling. Coming back, she had found a second rabbit out in the open and had coursed it, banking and swerving to intersect the line of retreat. He hadn't been ready and had reached her after she had settled down on her kill, broken the bones in its back legs and started to eat. To separate her from it he'd had to drop the leash on her neck repeatedly and talk to her soothingly before locking the collar and hauling her away. He'd left the carcass for the carrion-eaters.

It was his fourth day alone in the place and he could detect the rhythms he'd unwittingly imposed on his waking hours. It was going well. 'You won't meet a soul,' he'd been told. 'You won't hear a voice; likely enough, not even a car.' From the kitchen window he could see cattle grazing the sharply rising meadow above the house, sharing the pasture with two horses: a heavy dappled mare and a delicate, nervy-looking chestnut. From hour to hour they seemed to move no more than a dozen yards, the great drooping phalluses of neck and cheek continually browsing the slope.

After he'd thrown away the offal, he jointed the rabbit and began to slice some vegetables, talking to the dog as he worked.

The cab-driver was Polish and didn't much resemble his photograph. Idly, she guessed at variant pronunciations of his name, then turned to scrutinizing her notes as they drove the featureless turnpike. When the cab turned off East River Drive, however, bringing her at once into the city, she set the neatly typed pages aside and looked out with evident pleasure. They hit a massive pothole on the cross-town street, banging her spine. She almost laughed aloud. It was fun, being back.

She took out her diary and flipped through her next day's engagements: people she wanted to see; friends, dates to make for dinner or for the theatre later in the trip. Two weeks in the city, followed by four days in New England. She felt so relaxed that she permitted herself to imagine him next to her on the seat, his elbow jammed on the sill as always, his hand cupping his mouth, looking gloomily out at the billows of steam from gratings, the pretzel vendors, the endless cross-currents of people. As the cab drove alongside the park, a phalanx of rollerskaters left the sidewalk, airborne and crouching, then slalomed and jived through the crowd. She smiled and shook her head while her taxi bucketed down Fifth, rehearsing his bleak predictions. Perhaps she'd phone once she had settled in at the hotel.

'You assume you can walk through fire,' he would say, then insist on telling her some horror story from the newspapers or TV; he would recite the rape statistics. She wondered whether it were true: the propensity he found in her for risk-taking. Was it that she saw no risk – or considered that if it existed it threatened only other people? Was a sort of blindness involved? Arrogance? There were times when she thought that he alone could know, since he watched her so closely; but she was usually happy enough to join his speculation. She would theorize about herself, even be prepared to concede that this or that notion was a true one, but without wanting to examine too carefully the theory's constituents. Quite often, when he described a motive or unearthed some history, she would be eager to consider it; maybe it distracted her from whatever her own theories might have been. At times, though, she would curtail the vivisection of stratagems and silences. 'Don't say it . . . If I have to talk about things it becomes all the more difficult.' His reply was always the same: 'If we talk it can't change; if we don't it doesn't change; I may as well afford myself the luxury of letting you know how I feel.' Now and then she wanted him to be the stronger, but to become that he would have to fight her.

The upper windows of the high buildings were made glossy by the sun. The sky above them was flawless. When the cab stopped at a light, she saw a woman dressing one of several chic dummies in a vast shop-window. The model was just the taller of the two, its proportions moulded to excellence: slender white fingers extended crisply, thumbs and forefingers all but touching at the tips, the taut jawline, the exquisite pale features angled to direct its wide-eyed gaze down at the preoccupied face of the dresser who drew a silk blouse over its blind breasts, buttoning and arranging so that the merest swell stayed visible, nicely balanced in the shallow vee. It was bald and perfect. Hidden beneath the sweeping black full-length skirt, the neatly sloping curves and the two slanting lines that converged in the crotch to develop a tiny bulbousness were the guise of womanhood to make expensive clothes hang thus and thus, touch here, fall into a fold at just this point or that. Every impeccable line assisted it. The woman ran her hands, palms uppermost, under the long collar-points of the blouse to position it at the neck, then stood a little way back to observe before picking up a shawl and, with a wide flourish, throwing it behind the dummy's back and looping it either end across a crooked elbow; she settled it by drawing in some slack and arranging the drape. It was as if they were sisters, one happy to be cast in the role of curator. Selflessly she presented the other to the world – her irresistible handiwork.

114

As the cab drew away, she looked through the back window at the pair and saw that the woman's hands were resting on the dummy's waist: preparatory to moving it perhaps. She fantasized a bolt of tenderness passing between them.

The bell captain offloaded her luggage and wheeled it to the bank of lifts. The desk clerk greeted her like a friend who has been paid a welcome but unexpected visit and told her how great it was that she was back. He stamped an impression of her credit card on to the first page of her bill, then gave her the key to the suite she had asked them to reserve. After she had unpacked she decided to go down to Washington Square to watch the activity there; then, maybe, she'd treat herself to a cappuchino and a cream cake in Little Italy. 'Yes,' she said, rolling the names on her tongue.

Because he had to get up to fetch more logs he gave himself another whisky, coming back into the house by the side door that led to the kitchen, his load piled into the crook of one arm, and performing the whole operation one-handed: knocking ice out of the tray, unscrewing the bottle cap, pouring, tilting the soda syphon to bring the nozzle over the rim of the glass. He liked to pretend that it was an afterthought. He gulped some while walking through to the sitting-room, then set it down and tossed three logs on to the embers, stacking the rest alongside the grate. The wood caught at once, cracking loudly as it burned. A posse of insects scampered out from beneath a housing of bark, panicking this way and that before falling into the flames. The hound was lying full-length, bracketing the fire. She lifted her head, briefly, to check on the source of the noise, then lowered it, flexing her legs and groaning. The bark contracted as it singed; two circles, two weak-points, blackened and burned through – a mask's eyeholes rimmed with red. He sat for ten minutes, followed by another five; then he crossed to the desk and took the phone off the hook and left the room, making a double clicking sound with his tongue. The hound rose quickly, like a conspirator, and went past him to wait by the door.

Outside a wind was blowing. A few strings of rain floated towards him, silvered by the light from the window. They wandered the lanes for half-an-hour. At one point they stopped close by a cedar that was silhouetted against the paler sky and waited until a strong gust came so that he could watch, eyes half closed, as it appeared to rotate – a trick learned in childhood. He'd overdone it once in a garden ringed by cedars, going out at dusk and standing in the centre of the lawn by the hole of the clock-golf course and turning through the hours to face each tree in turn. He'd crashed down on his back with no notion that he was going to fall. The adults had witnessed only his collapse. Too dizzy to walk, he'd been carried indoors and clucked over and asked interminably if he felt sick or had banged his head. There seemed to be no explanation he could give them.

He towelled his hair and returned the phone to its cradle. He decided on a nightcap and drank it standing up in the kitchen. He looked into every room before going to bed, to make sure that things were as they should be.

By chance, because she wandered where she did, the order was reversed: coffee first, in a chrome-and-mirrors restaurant crowded with loud families, then to Washington Square to watch the freak-show. She had become suddenly tired, though, and did no more than walk slowly round the perimeter before flagging a taxi. She felt happy, but the journey had begun to tell on her – gritty eyes, a touch of lightheadedness.

She'd been planning on a movie but decided, instead, to call room service for an early supper and watch television for an hour or so. Before all that she'd have a bath. Long ago she had decided that hotel rooms were wonderful: luxury would be to live permanently in a suite like this one. Steam from the bathroom furled round the lintel of the connecting door as she sat on the bed and eased her boots off. Half undressed, she lounged back on her elbows, pressing the TV 'on' button with her toe. A preacher was stalking the stage of a packed hall, shaking a Bible fiercely at his audience so that the pages flopped and fluttered; his voice was now a whisper, now an anguished howl; his face gleamed with tears. The novelty delighted her.

She eased into her bath, sinking up to her neck, and her muscles slackened; she sighed, resting her head against the rim, then reached over the side to retrieve the room service menu that she'd carried in with her. Consommé, omelette, a salad with blue-cheese dressing. A bottle of Chablis which they would bring in an ice bucket clouded with condensation. The heavy white tablecloth and napkin. The tumbler of iced water with its scalloped cardboard lid. The posy in a waisted glass.

She dropped the card and brought her arms into the bath and under the water so that her hands fell into her lap. Her eyes closed. She started a gentle rocking motion with her pelvis to make the bathwater run over her in tiny waves. As she rocked she began to think through her first couple of appointments, but abandoned that as she grew drowsy. A wave ticked on her chin. She rocked almost imperceptibly to keep them going, imagining her body hair switching back and forth in the current like a sea-growth, and her labia pursing in frills underwater: a mollusc with its slow, even undulations, loosely pink. She stroked herself with the length of a finger for the small sensation it would bring, then sighed again and sat up to wash off the grime of airports and the celebrated toxic particles.

When he woke at dawn, she was still up, despite her tiredness. She lay on her stomach, feet under a pillow, chin propped in cupped hands, watching her second feature film on cable TV. It wasn't until two o'clock that she switched off and lay in the darkness listening to the hollow *whoop-whoop-whoop* of squad cars going up Sixth. From time to time during the night she came awake and they were always there, sometimes close, sometimes distant, the city's owls.

One side of the valley had the sun, the other was stark white with frost. The dog stopped when he stopped and lay down when he lay down, edging her chest on to a corner of his waterproof. He lifted his face to the sun and beneath his closed eyelids lozenges of white and red orbited in blackness. When, five minutes later, he opened them and viewed the opposite slope, a combination of the light on his retina and the shaded expanse of frost made the scene appear in violent negative; in the instant that he looked, the entire acreage seemed to leap towards him and hover.

It would be easy, he thought, to flirt with foolish concepts of the numinous in nature and smiled at his susceptibility. Fifty or so sheep were grazing a long meadow on the far side, their backs marked with red and blue blotches – an undignified branding that made them already meat. He looked beyond them, left and right, trying to pinpoint the terrain his dream had used, not knowing the ground well enough to be able to decide whether it existed or was merely an all-purpose dream-landscape.

The rabbit had become a fox and she had disabled it without finishing it, coursing over open ground: though when he'd gone close to make the kill it had lain in a narrow track, belly-down in the mud, looking rather like the silk-lined pelt his mother had worn for special occasions. High on its back, the rufous fur had been laid open; the flesh too, exposing the spine which had the appearance of a chicken's leg-bone after the cooked carcass has gone cold: a dry, grey stick. He took a stone to break it, but couldn't get an angle inside the wound. He laboured away, straddling the creature and stabbing ineffectually. Shortly, a rider drew up behind: he was blocking the path. Discountenanced, he pounded all the harder, but it was no good, so finally he moved the beast to one side in order to continue his work there. She looked down wordlessly as she passed. She was wearing her new stock-pin and a bowler – very correct – that he'd never seen her in before.

It wouldn't decode. The recollection of his mother's fox fur was probably a red herring, though he now remembered very precisely the glass discs for eyes and the tortoiseshell clip that fastened the snout to the base of the tail. No words had passed between them. He wondered whether she had recognized him.

The hound rose to some small movement on the valley floor and stared fixedly at one section of hedgerow close to the stream. After a while the pose broke and she began to trot back and forth on the hill's flank – little meanderings as she took one scent or another – and paused to glance about her from time to time. When she sighted new prey she leapt off at once, long back legs thrusting against the turf to put her into full flight. He watched her sleekness as it flowed downhill. She hurdled the low hedge and veered left, sprinting up an incline towards a patch of gorse.

He followed her, backtracking along the line of the valley and calling as he walked. She reappeared in the field closest to home, bringing with her a brown-and-white terrier that pattered along behind looking eager. 'Well, well,' he said, 'where did you spring from? Go home.' He swung the leash at it. 'Go on home.' It ignored him and continued to follow, taking a blow or two from the bony hind legs as it craned to sniff the bitch's rump. When she crouched, the smaller dog got its muzzle under her tail and lapped at the stream of piss. He yelled and it half straightened, looking towards him, its teeth chattering with pleasure. He flung the leash and both dogs skittered, the terrier finally retreating after having left its spoor on top of hers. She went to heel when he ordered it. As they neared the house, he began to plan the day.

The noise came first: a high-pitched rumble that intensified as she ascended the short flight of stairs and, when she neared the room, seemed to grow more rapid in its fluctuations. Standing in the doorway she could detect other, lesser, sounds: glasses chiming irregularly as they were carried about the room on trays, a champagne cork coming free, laughter that seemed to run a zig-zag course from one group to another.

She looked forward to joining in. Ed Kowalski found her before she'd taken more than a couple of steps into the room, arriving at her side with two full glasses and pecking at the cheek she offered. 'I'm so glad you were able to come. I imagine you know lots of these people.' He extended an arm and moved his champagne glass in a wide semicircle.

'I expect so,' she said. 'I'll tell you when I get a bit closer. It's vain of me not to wear my glasses.' Ed laughed and began to chat to her about their profession, the new gossip, the pending deals. They both thought she looked good. The dress was new; but since nothing she wore ever looked like either a recent purchase or an old favourite, only its elegance and fit were apparent. It clung, but wasn't tight. A symmetrical concavity rose to either hip bone and the line from these points swept down to her calves, perfectly tailored. Her breasts made just the right balance; their slight movement as she walked was part of the design's logic and the material's purpose. Although she was slim, she had dieted to lose almost half a stone during the weeks preceding the trip.

Ed released her to circulate and she spent two hours moving from question to question, answer to answer, saying much the same thing each time, though with no sense of tedium. Business dates were made for later that week. Everyone remarked on how well she seemed; most of the men added that she was beautiful – offering the compliment as a kind of greeting. Later, at dinner, Ed told her the same thing and she thanked him. It pleased her when she noticed that he was eyeing her as she gave her order to the waiter and again as she ransacked her bag for cigarettes. It pleased her that he would make a pass which she would gently deflect before returning, alone, to her hotel. He was an attractive man and speculation amused her. It pleased her, in part, because it would be a harmless secret.

A poached cock-pheasant hung from a pipe in the scullery. He'd spotted it pecking at the lawn, expecting the garden to be safe ground, he supposed, since the house was often empty. Easing open an upstairs window, he had rested a ·22 air rifle on the sill and picked off the bird with a head-shot. Each time the hound went in there she stood on her hind legs to nuzzle it. Tapping her shoulder, he said, 'Down.' The pheasant revolved to face him and he thought how gormless it looked, its thin, flat beak half parted as if it were about to emit the goofy cackle of some cartoon character. The eyes were cataracted in death and a small globule of blood lay on its cheek. It had been a particularly good shot and he would have liked to have been able to tell someone about it. A handful of corn cast on the lawn, he reflected, might bring interesting results.

He prepared the dog's food and waited while she ate, then led her out of the scullery and secured the door. He didn't bother to cook anything for himself; instead, he took a bottle of Scotch into the drawing-room and placed it on the desk, then crossed to the fireside armchair and picked up a novel that lay open on the seat. By eight-thirty he'd read a chapter, so he went to the kitchen and brought back a glass which he set next to the bottle. After the next, which he read with a concentrated care that involved a refusal to allow any passage to be scanned for its narrative drift alone, he went out again and returned with the soda. In a chapter's time he would get a drink. On the desk, in a precise line, stood syphon, glass, whisky, the telephone, his address book, a box of ·22 slugs and the journal he was failing to keep. He turned a page with one finger of the hand that held the book; the other lay lightly on the hound's dome. He fondled her ears and she leaned into the motion. He progressed patiently from paragraph to paragraph.

By the morning of the fifth day it was becoming hard work and she had begun to think about the weekend as a kind of therapy. Even so, it hadn't stopped being enjoyable. They had been to the theatre, to a small drinks party given in her honour and to some very good restaurants. Ed had been consistently thoughtful; and he accepted that it had been necessary for her to arrange dinner dates with other business contacts for most of the following week. He'd wondered whether she might like to take the Circle Line trip round the island on Saturday; she'd said she might. It was clear that she must judge her responses accurately.

She stole the afternoon in order to go shopping with a girlfriend whose marriage had moved her to the city five years before. They spent three hours in Bloomingdale's, then went back to the hotel and had a drink in the bar. She had been seen passing the reception desk and a bell-boy came up to their table clutching a wad of telexes and messages written on the hotel's printed forms. Her friend laughed. 'It certainly makes my life seem dull,' she said, and took the hint to leave.

The desk clerk raised a hand in salute as she crossed the lobby; she waved back, using the hand that clutched the messages so that he would know she'd got them. Once in the lift she began to thumb through the telephone messages and realized that she was looking for his name. Everything would need to be replied to that day. She was reading a long telex from her office when the lift stopped. Two men in the corridor parted to permit her to step between them. She looked up briefly to orientate herself and muttered, 'Thanks,' then continued down the corridor, still reading.

Her room was the last on the left. When she slotted the key in, the door moved forward: it hadn't caught properly; maybe it had failed to click into place, or it might have been that the locking nib was in need of oil and hadn't returned when the handle had been released; these were the causes that occurred to her afterwards. She went in and turned towards where the couch and coffee table in her own suite would have been. There were two people in the room: a man of about fifty and a woman who was probably in her twenties. They were seated on an upright chair facing a long mirror that was fixed to the wall. Their backs were towards her. It was their reflection she saw, her reflection that they both looked up to as the door opened and she stepped into view behind them. The woman was sitting four-square on the man's lap, facing directly ahead; he was looking round her left shoulder at their images in the long glass. He was clothed, she naked; and she sat astride, her thighs at a wider angle to his. In order to stretch her further, the man had wound his lower legs round hers and braced an instep on each of her calves and was levering outwards. She was so forked that she might have tipped forward had he not wrapped one broad, shirtsleeved forearm round her waist. His other arm was bent at the elbow and pointing downward: a delicately contrived angle. His fingers were at her crotch, two extended, two drawn back, like a harpist's.

She thought she might have said, 'Oh . . .', certainly not more than that, before turning swiftly. In her anxiety to get out she half collided with the door, dropping her messages, but scooped them up in a second, crouching and rising and drawing the door after her in one continuous motion, then walked briskly towards the lift, starting to trot when it didn't come into sight as soon as she'd expected. She poked the button, looking sometimes back down the corridor, sometimes at the numerals as they glowed in order of ascendance. It occurred to her that she must have paused for a time to have been able to observe all that she had, though she was only aware of having entered, seen, and retreated. What she remembered most was the arm that had been reaching down, the shirt-cuff folded back to reveal thick striations of black hair like bangles. He'd been balding: a meaty face and brow. He, or perhaps the girl, had twisted her long hair into a hank and thrown it over her right shoulder to leave his view unimpeded. They had lifted their heads quickly and in unison, like creatures disturbed at their feeding.

In her own room she tossed the fistful of papers down on the coffee table and laughed sharply, then shuddered. The television offered three news broadcasts – one in Spanish, a sit-com, some re-runs of old movies, a quiz game in which people dressed as chickens cavorted and scored points. She sat on the arm of the couch to watch, glancing now and then at the unanswered messages. An hour later, as she emerged from the shower, she realized she'd left a shopping-bag in the bar, and phoned the desk to instruct them to give it to Mr Kowalski who could bring it up when he called to collect her for the theatre.

*

'That was so nice. You have been kind.' She leaned across in the back of the cab to kiss Ed goodnight, patting his hand fondly. He looked rueful and smiled his unasked question. She smiled back knowingly but lowered her eyes in refusal, telling herself not to weaken.

They had eaten dinner but she felt hungry: perhaps there had been too much fencing during the evening; whatever the reason, she had ordered unwisely and hadn't much wanted the food. Ed's ploys hadn't upset her, of course – the way he'd taken her arm as they walked: a little high, so that his knuckles would rub her breast; his fingertips on her neck, briefly, when he'd helped her out of her coat – but they had been a distraction. After his cab had gone she went into the bar to ask whether room service would bring her a sandwich but, as she'd suspected, it was too late. The barman shrugged and raised his hands palms upward. He was serving drinks to three hookers who perched on bar stools, chatting like shift-workers in the staff canteen. The girl nearest to her swivelled on her stool and pointed towards the street. 'There's a deli on the next block: corner of Sixth.'

Once she'd been reminded she couldn't resist the notion: a huge sandwich with little canisters of pickle and relish, a milkshake. She walked swiftly – not at all apprehensive, but eager to buy the tuck and return to her room for half-an-hour's TV, followed by a bath and some virtuous writing up of notes in the queen-sized bed which she would finally occupy by stretching from corner to corner in the moment when her thoughts began to edge into and out of coherence and her body was drawn down by the warmth.

The delicatessen was big and brightly lit. Four broad steps led down to its double doors. On the third a man was lying face down, his left leg trailing over the lowest step so that two customers, making for the street with their bags and cartons of coffee, had to step first over the leg, then the torso. It was plain that he was a vagrant. His clothes were filthy, ragged and ill-fitting. What she could see of his face was seamed with dirty grey stubble. Shards of glass and a bottle neck lay on the steps and the area stank of liquor. Kneeling beside him was a man who wore a long white apron and a white cardboard trilby; his fingers were pressed to the vagrant's neck. People went to and fro from street to door and back. Beyond the plate-glass window, other aprons and trilbys spooned and sliced and poured and handed paper bags across the counter. A fog of steam surrounded the coffee machine and dampened the glass.

She stared down at her little adventure. The man in the apron spoke to her, perhaps to reassure. 'We've called the para-medics. I think he's dead, though. Can't get a pulse here.' He shifted his fingers slightly as if to demonstrate his eagerness to track down some errant flutter. His hat, and the skirt of his apron, held a pale blue glow: light from the neon script that burned above the door. She glanced up to check the name before stepping over the tatty sack of limbs. It wasn't clear what happened after that.

'Your voice sounds . . . I don't know . . . unused.'

'Yes? Well, I haven't spoken to anyone for more than a week. Except the dog.'

'How is it?'

'Fine. A trifle dull, perhaps. It really is isolated here. I shot a pheasant.'

'What on earth with?'

'The ·22. Bloody good shot: right into the head. It was wandering about on the back lawn, pecking like some old hen. *Bap!* It's hanging in the scullery.'

'Whose was it?'

'Christ knows. How's it with you?'

'Fine. I'm having a good time. Busy.'

'Parties and suchlike?'

'No, no. Nothing like that. Work. The hatchings of deals in *nouvelle cuisine* restaurants.'

'Plaited asparagus drenched in goo; litres of Perrier.' ·

'Very like that, yes.'

'What about the evenings? Have you been to any theatre?'

'Last Thursday with Lucy. I told you I'd be seeing her, didn't I?'

'Yes. You were going to play hookey.'

'We wound up in Bloomingdale's. Credit cards flashed like the Saracen sword.'

'I thought you might. What did you see?'

'Oh – in the Village – you know Lucy. Something extravagantly allusive; I've forgotten the name. A sort of Greek chorus stood on a raised dais at the back of the stage singing in E-flat while the actors wandered through the audience miming existential crises. It was quite fun actually; I mean, not the usual thing. There's a crêperie opened up on Bleeker Street. We went there afterwards. She thinks she might be getting a divorce.'

'You mean she's not sure?'

'Opinions differ about its desirability.'

'Between her and Michael?'

'That's right.'

'She's for, he's against.'

'Exactly.'

'What about that Ed Whatsit who fancies you?'

'Nonsense.'

'Sure he does. Unctuous bastard. They had to employ extra bell-boys to carry the flowers, I recall.'

'I gave him a good tip-off. They were very nice flowers.'

'Made the place smell like a chapel of rest.'

'I'm seeing him next Wednesday, I think.'

'Dinner, I imagine.'

'Lunch. Look, I'm too tired to . . .'

'It's going all right then; you're pleased?'

'So far, yes. I'm looking forward to New England.'

'Give them my love.'

'Yes. It's another week yet.'

'How's the hotel?'

'Utterly unchanged. I'm on the fourteenth floor. I suppose I ought . . .'

'Your mother called.'

'Oh?'

'Just to . . . you know. They're fine.'

'Well, I haven't had time, really, to phone anyone.'

'No. I'll let them know you called.'

'Would you? Thanks. I'd better . . .'

'It's bloody cold here. I've had the fires going all day. Winter's starting. My little domestic routines . . . fetch the coal, walk the dog, open a tin. Work, read. A model of hermitry.'

'It sounds idyllic.'

'It's cold there, I imagine.'

'Outside, very. Inside, Saharan. You know how they overdo it. Actually, I'm expecting the desk to phone; someone's calling to see me.'

'Anyone fun?'

'No. Someone's two-i-c.'

'Okay. I must take the dog out. I know what I wanted to ask you: what's the name of that deli we used to go to sometimes – not far?'

'Joy's.'

'Joy's Deli. Of course it is.'

'I think I'll have to go. They're probably trying to call me.'

'Sure. You'll let me know about plane times and so forth? So that I can allow for fog, bad traffic, civil disturbances, acts of God . . . ?'

'Yes,' she said. 'That seems a long way off.'

The afternoon was blowy, the sky full of fast clouds. A faint green flexing light seemed to lie over everything, as if refracted through a lens, appearing to narrow and widen in shifting beams as the wind blew, bringing horizons closer, throwing into the middle distance objects near at hand. He trudged the crevice of the valley with the dog loping at his side. His route would take him across two hills and on through a pine forest, climbing again to a ruined folly – a mock-Gothic landmark – built at the highest point in the area; he'd be back at the right time for his first drink.

After they had gone two miles the rain came up behind him, a faint drubbing on the yoke of his oilskin, and he hunched his shoulders to it. As he walked he sent her back to the neon-washed steps of Joy's Deli, to take up where she had left off.

THE FIFTH YEAR

*

July

He woke feeling well: clear-headed and not at all sluggish. The shutters had been folded back and the room was bright with sunlight. From what he could see of it, the sky was cloudless. It was their first fine weather for twelve days. During the initial seconds of wakefulness, he registered these things – his untypical alertness, the sunlight, the sky. Then he felt the peppery heat under the bridge of his nose and tasted his mouth. He realized that his stomach was shrunken and sour. A headache started up over the right eye and began to soak in. He knew the signs. There would be another five minutes of manageable but mounting discomfort, then the hangover would hit.

He recalled that he'd been drinking *marc* and knew that he wouldn't get off lightly. He'd bought the bottle three days before in the general store that they'd taken to using for just about everything. The owner had seen him pondering the display of liqueurs and had come over. He'd already made it plain that he didn't speak much French, so the man had yelled baby-phrases at him and wagged the bottle by its neck, tapping the label and rolling his eyes. 'C'est très fort; très bon.' A flexed bicep had indicated that here was a *man's* drink. He was so taken with the shopkeeper's enthusiasm that he'd replaced the brandy he'd chosen and put the *marc* into his wire basket along with a few litres of wine. It had been evident that this substitution hadn't been reckoned on: the man's smile had wilted and his eyes had gone from the brandy – restored to the shelf – and the less expensive *marc*. He'd said, 'Ah . . .', as if about to explain the mistake, then retreated to the counter, speaking to himself in a rapid undertone.

The bad weather had kept them in. Neither felt inclined to make a trip to the town for shopping unless it was essential.

131

After two days the *marc* had been all that was left in the house. They'd had their first drink at about six-thirty, after he'd hauled in two basketsful of logs and lit the fire. She'd been sleeping in an armchair, under a blanket, arms folded against the evening chill. As the kindling had begun to catch and crackle she'd peered over the tasselled fringe and said, 'Oh good.'

'Yes and no,' he'd told her. 'This is pretty much the last of the wood.'

'We've used the lot?'

'Very nearly.' He'd added some small logs. 'There might be another basketful.'

'How embarrassing. It was probably their winter supply. What shall we do?'

'Drive to Spain, perhaps. Let's try some of that *marc*.' He'd stood up and slapped his hands against one another to clean them before fetching the bottle. Her first swallow had made her cough and wave her fingers in front of her mouth.

'Firewater,' she'd said hoarsely.

The symptoms deepened. Little gushers of bile rose and fell, making his stomach clench. The pain behind his eyes was so bad, now, that his head nodded to its beat. Each time he was appalled at how grossly ill he became. Other people were able to be rueful about their hangovers – were able to function, afflicted by nothing more than the kind of sore-headedness that makes jokes of inadvertently slammed doors or thoughtlessly raised voices. Clownish and wry, they managed to bring a certain style to their suffering. What he endured bore no trace of the romantic. It was humiliating and grimy; its odours were indelible; it came laden with guilt and self-loathing.

He lay still for fifteen minutes, whimpering and talking out loud as if trying some incantation. Finally, a backwash of nausea broke in his throat and he went, with a quick, stiff-legged walk, to the bathroom and knelt in front of the lavatory bowl – the drunk's proper obeisance. Between each throat-wrenching rush he sat back on his heels, letting his forehead rest on the porcelain

rim, and repeated the silly, trite litany: *never again, never again.*
He got back to bed draped over his own arm, sweating and
quaking. He felt weaker and slightly recovered. The weakness
would increase and the sense of recovery lessen while the cycle
moved towards another attack. As his face neared the pillow, he
recoiled from the hot, saline dampness he'd left there. Fragments
of recollection began to torment him. He yelped as if stung. A
series of tableaux, increasingly shameful, assembled and dis-
solved before his mind's eye. In one, he was telling some
extravagant lie, harmless except for her disbelief. In another, he
had grown unstoppably garrulous; she was sitting close to the
fire, her legs drawn up under her, trying to find some well of
thought in which his voice might become soluble. Then he was
crouching next to her, much too close, wanting to give her
another drink. Tension was visible in every line, every angle of
her body. The booze had loosened his features and made them
coarse. She was twisting a spike of hair with the first two fingers
of one hand, a continuous rotation, though she was scarcely
aware of doing it. He'd pursued her glass with the bottle neck
and another image had him sprawling across her lap. Her arm,
outstretched to keep the glass out of reach, had drawn him on
and drunkenness had toppled him.

He couldn't remember what had made him angry; he supposed it to have been some fabrication or another – her tone of
voice or some misinterpreted remark. At times it seemed they
spoke to one another in a recondite, courtly language which
required that each comment, each response, be decoded. It
sounded innocuous enough, but its underside was heavily
mined. A wrong inflexion, an unguarded reply, could produce
a chain-reaction from which there was no retreat. As he fell on
her, he lost control of the bottle and soaked her sleeve. She
heaved her thighs sideways to throw him off and he crashed
into the hearth, scattering the andirons. Her face was ferocious
with distaste.

He fixed himself in that pose: a grotesque, a reveller tipped on
his arse with arms flung out and the bottle gripped by the neck

– a detail from an etching by Hogarth – and shook his head as if that might dislodge the memory. On his way to the bathroom again he remembered something she had said; then his mind emptied as the awful heaving began – so violent that it seemed to haul his stomach against his backbone. He shuffled back to bed, one hand against the wall as he went, and lay there breathing shallowly, listening. There was birdsong, the mono-tone of crickets, the occasional burp from some tree-frogs that had taken refuge in the cellar.

It was before he'd lost his balance and splashed her sleeve. Her body was turned, defensively. She said, 'Your voice is like white noise. If you hooded me and went on as you do, I'd start to hallucinate.'

'You don't listen,' he said. 'You deflect things. I could talk for hours and still barely get the rind off what I want to say.'

She raised both hands – an exaggerated shrug. In one of them was her drink and she took a small sip. 'I listen; I hear; I don't always feel the need to comment.'

'Ladylike reticence?' He answered himself. 'No. Queenly disdain.'

'If you like,' she sighed. 'It's not so, but if you like.'

'How patronizing,' he said. 'How perfectly judged. Who else could intimidate and provoke at the same time? You're a fucking artist, you know. Such artistry.' And he poured himself a drink with a fancy flourish.

There must have been a lull. He remembered which records he'd played and the book he'd leafed through. They had fed the fire and kept silence for a while. He was looking up from the page to watch her as she watched the flames and saw a face wiped of all expression, void, as if some vacuum – hope in abeyance perhaps – had siphoned off her passing thoughts.

By noon he'd thrown up eleven times. The headache had ebbed – he thought of it that way, imagining his brain's undulations wet and dense, like sandflats. In the main room things had been tidied up: bottle, glasses, the dishes from their evening meal; the ashtrays had been emptied, the hearth swept. On the table was a beer-mug holding a bunch of garden flowers. It wouldn't have been surprising to have found her outside in the egg-shaped wicker chair that hung from a branch of a tree, but as he was leaving the house he noticed that the car had gone. A heat haze rose from the far fields, warping the view. The sun was astonishingly hot. He felt peeled and slightly sticky.

The house was built on a steep slope, isolated by woodland and scrub. From where he stood he could look down on the valley's thickets, then across to farmland and the farm's few buildings – their nearest neighbour. He saw a length of stream and the strip of the metalled road she would have taken. When he reached the wicker chair he knelt on hands and knees in the grass and was sick for the last time. Soon he'd begin to recover. There would be two or three hours of feeling maudlin and faintly horny; after that he'd grow hungry, then pleasantly tired. Sitting in the chair, using one heel to keep it swinging back and forth, he formed a picture of himself rising from the hearth and taking a swipe at her which missed because it was meant to. She didn't see it. Her eyes were shut and her hands over her ears. Most of the rest was missing. All he could get was a batch of random images. It wasn't even certain that they all came from the previous evening.

They were waltzing in the space between armchairs and dining-table, laughing because they didn't really know the steps. They one-two-three'd up and down, bumping knees and miming the smooth smiles of professionals.

She was writing postcards while he lit the oil lamps – two on the table, two on a stone shelf above the hearth. A ribbon of dark smoke rose from each until he lowered the wick.

They were screeching at one another, their faces lopsided with spite and reddened by the fire's glow. He was pointing a finger as if to single her out – the culprit! Own up!

She stood with her back to him, undressing for bed. He appeared to be sleeping, but was not. She took off this and that, adroitly, like someone alone. Then she stopped to examine the inside of one thigh. She whispered a *Damn*, reaching for a tissue.

In going towards the window, he fell against the dining-table and then to the floor. Why was he going to the window? His glass shot from his hand and shattered. He lay like one crucified and must have dozed. When he woke, she was asleep in her chair.

There were many blank passages. There were moments that couldn't be placed in sequence. The window was a black square beyond which appeared his reflection and the room's, blurred, as if their outlines had begun to seep, and trembling slightly when a wind shook the glass. The picture was two-dimensional. Some object on a shelf behind him seemed to sit on his shoulder like an imp.

She was smiling as he told the story of how he'd come to buy the *marc*.

He went back to the bedroom and sat on a kitchen stool that she had placed beside the tall chest of drawers. At eye-level on the chest were a small, oval mirror, a hairbrush, nail scissors, bits and pieces of make-up, some tubes and pots of lotion, a perfume atomizer. Near by was a waste-bin. He found the tissue. It bore one stiff, almost circular stain near its centre, together with some paler streaks and smudges. He made a ball of it, rolling each corner inwards by turns so that the heavy stain was outermost. Next he unpicked all the hairs from the bristles of her brush, separating each strand and laying them side by side on the polished top of the chest. By revolving them between finger and thumb he made a little rope which he knotted at both ends, then tied it round the tissue.

The headache had gone completely, but he felt brittle – a bird-boned arrangement of thin limbs, and skin like shellac. Giddiness came and went; crossing the room he felt for each step forward as if he might encounter a sudden slope. He crouched by their open suitcase and found the jacket that contained his wallet. In one of the compartments was a tiny photograph – one of four she'd taken in a booth. Its sister was in her passport. There was also a letter with *January 4th* written beneath a hotel's printed heading, but giving no year.

There isn't much snow – not enough anyway, so for the last two days we've been sight-seeing. The ski-bums spend most of their time looking at the sky, like members of some Alpine cargo-cult, and nodding sagely. They say it's on the way. The crowd in the chalet are okay – a bit dull perhaps. James and Anna asked me to send their regards. I hope it does snow soon. I'm always terrified, of course, but it *is* exciting – and I've too much time to brood. I *wish* you could have come. I miss you. I keep wanting to ask you things. (Later) – We had dinner and went to a rather pleasantly tatty nightclub populated by package tours and predatory ski-instructors. It started to snow really quite hard about three hours ago and shows no sign of letting up, so perhaps I'll be on the slopes tomorrow . . .

He used the nail scissors to cut out the endearment and her signature, then pushed the oblong of paper and the photograph under the binding of hair. In the kitchen he came up with a small plastic bag containing a few olives. He emptied the olives on to a saucer, then washed and dried the bag before dropping his gleanings into it and knotting the top. He put the bag into the zipper compartment of his wallet and the wallet back into his coat pocket. That done, he found his binoculars and went out to the wicker chair.

The strip of road stayed empty. Sunlight whitened it so that at times you might have thought it was water. He shopped around with the glasses, but the view didn't yield much. There was no remnant of the days of rain. Everything was dry and warm to the touch. 'Why speculate?' he thought; even so, a pang of alarm struck him and the headache threatened again.

The glasses showed him a flock of geese in the farmyard below and a cat stalking something close to a barn wall. He switched to the farmhouse, going from window to window, and was rewarded with a slight movement on the upper storey. He held steady on the place and saw someone pass back and forth several times – almost certainly a woman, but she wouldn't keep still. It was difficult to say what her purpose might have been. Now and then she stooped, always at the same point; she could have been filling a suitcase, or peering into a mirror, or testing a child's fever.

Seconds later he found the hawk. It glided low over the farmhouse roof, then peeled off to the right so that he had to lower the glasses to pinpoint it – above a wheatfield where it hovered minute after minute, so that his forearms began to ache with the effort of keeping the binoculars positioned. He looked for so long that the bird and the clear disc of sky seemed cut off from all else – a medallion, or a seal, with the hawk in bas-relief. As he watched it slipped sideways, felt the airstream for a moment more, then began to fly directly towards him, its sickle-shaped wings flickering. He adjusted the focus to follow it and eased out of the chair. He was looking almost straight up when the hawk stalled and went into a dive, appearing to take a perfect line for his face, as if it were flying down a tunnel of air circumscribed by the glasses. He was transfixed, watching it come until it filled his vision and he let the binoculars fall and flung up an arm, crying out and turning his head from the impact.

It really hadn't been that close – tree-top height perhaps, and in a trajectory that would have ended on the far side of the house beyond the wood-store. He clucked his tongue, like a nurse admonishing a troublesome patient, and examined the binoculars for damage. They looked intact, but he tested them to be sure and in doing so picked up the car as it turned off the road and began to climb the narrow track that led up to the house.

She had brought provisions for about three days. One bag held pâté, eggs, several different kinds of sausage, salad and vegetables, a chicken, two baguettes, whisky and wine, some steaks for a treat. He took the items from her as they were unloaded and shuffled round the kitchen putting them in their right places. Near the town was a small artists' colony – that was how it advertised itself. She'd been to look and showed him a bracelet decorated with heavy, pale blue stones, lozenge-shaped and set in silver.

Lodged in the top of the second bag was a small cardboard box with a blue cross stencilled on it. 'Aspirin,' she said, handing it to him. 'You know how to use them?'

'I'm led to believe that you shove them up your arse.'

'Indeed you do.' She smiled, arranging other purchases on the table. 'How are you feeling?'

He held one hand out, palm down, and rocked it.

She said: 'Bad luck. I thought you might. What did you do this morning?'

'Slept a bit. Lay around praying for death.'

'Mmmm . . .' She frowned, looking along the kitchen shelves, then found the pasta jar she was seeking and poured noodles into it, just managing to empty the packet. 'Have you eaten anything?'

He shook his head.

'But you're hungry.'

'I will be.'

'Let's have the chicken,' she suggested, 'with some broccoli. I thought I might attempt a hollandaise sauce.' She moved from place to place, collecting ingredients and utensils, humming a melody – the song they had played while trying to waltz. As she worked she chatted to him about the artists and their spick-and-span workshops. The half-dozen cobbled streets, she said, had been sluiced and scrubbed. The silversmiths, painters and potters sat outside their shops and drank coffee, waiting patiently for customers. You gained the impression that everything was miniaturized, even the people, like a model village. He thought that he had never seen her do this before: she had never chopped and poured and mixed, talking easily to him all the time; had never occupied a kitchen with this sort of leisurely confidence.

139

'On my way back,' she said, 'driving down the hill from the artists . . . it was extraordinary – I saw what I would have sworn was a wolf.'

'Impossible,' he said. 'Where?'

'On the road. There were woods on both sides. It crossed over and went in among the trees. I was quite close to it.'

'Impossible.'

'I know. Obviously, it was a dog. But you know what a wolf looks like? It looked like that. Not at all like a dog. Like a wolf you see in the zoo.'

'It must have been the last wolf in France. Did you stop?'

'Well, slowed down, you know, but it had gone.'

He said: 'No. An Alsatian or whatever. Some sort of unlikely cross-breed.'

'Oh yes,' she agreed. 'It looked exactly like a wolf.' She lit the oven and put the chicken inside. 'Okay,' she said. 'Done. Thank God for this weather.'

He spread a blanket for her, then lowered himself on to the wicker chair, resting the binoculars on his lap. A little later she emerged with book, dark glasses and sun-tan oil. She undressed and lay at his feet. He felt sad but not depressed – weepy, which was nothing more than the hangover following its course. The sun had struck the farmhouse windows, seven patches of solid light, so he quartered the farmyard and the fields beyond, but found nothing.

'Don't the French maintain that a menstruating woman shouldn't be allowed to make hollandaise?' he asked. 'Something to do with the constituents refusing to blend?'

'Yes.' She looked taken aback. 'How do you know that?'

'Someone told me. Can't remember.'

She turned over and picked up her book. 'Maybe you should do it.'

'No – let's fly in the face of tradition. Let's put the old wives to the test.'

'What can you see?' She shaded her eyes briefly and looked down towards the road.

'Nothing.'

'Not my wolf?'

'Afraid not. I expect he's out there somewhere, trying to avoid extinction.'

'What would he live off do you think?'

'Old wives,' he said. 'Lost children, unwary ramblers.'

'Watercolourists venturing outside the colony in search of the picturesque.'

'Just an hors d'oeuvre.'

'Doesn't anyone miss them?'

'It's one of the region's enduring mysteries.'

'Poor old sod,' she said. 'Good luck to him.'

Her wolf would become a topic, he realized, good for some anthropomorphic flights of fancy over the next few days. He remembered why he had tried to give her that drink, the one he'd poured on her arm, and although he realized that he'd been prompted by a drunkard's fractured reasoning, he wondered whether he ought to let her know that there had, at least, been a purpose to it. He decided to let it go. It would be difficult to make her believe that some virtue had been squandered. Instead, he focussed the glasses on the farm and fields again, picking out landmarks for the story he would tell her about the wolf.

When she put down her book half-an-hour later he was asleep, his face pressed against the chair's lattice-work. She got up and put on her dress – it would have felt odd to cook while naked – then reached out and gave him a gentle nudge, not to wake him but to set the chair rocking, very slightly, on its rope. The wicker made a just audible noise: *mew, mew, mew*. Using the tips of her fingers, she kept the chair in motion, pushing him as if he were an infant on a swing. Her head was to one side and she stared unblinkingly at a featureless patch of grass. A breeze turned the pages of her book. 'Well,' she spoke softly to herself, 'let's tackle this hollandaise.' She gave him a last push for luck and went towards the house, walking unsteadily because she'd been in the sun.

THE FIFTH YEAR

*

10 September–16 September

He thought: *Standing in the doorway, he lit a cigarette and sifted through the faces. He wanted to appear neither incurious nor eager.* A moment earlier, Elaine Mason had opened the front door to him, taken his coat, and equipped him with a drink. 'The food's almost gone,' she'd told him, 'but there's still plenty of this. How are you?' and they'd chatted for a time, standing in the kitchen with some of the party's overspill, until she'd taken some bottles of wine from the fridge and begun to shoulder her way into the crowded drawing-room.

Standing in the doorway he lit a cigarette and sifted through the faces. He wanted to appear neither incurious nor eager. He found her in a small group standing by an open window. Streamers of smoke floated towards the draught, eddying briefly as they met the cool air, then whipping round the frame in little billows of white. She was listening and smiling; you could lip-read her intermittent, 'Yes . . . yes . . .' He recognized the likeableness that made her so popular – in part, a talent for showing enthusiasm, for being able to help maintain a balanced conversation. She was keeping her cigarette stub vertical to preserve the long column of ash. When she was no longer being spoken to directly she turned aside to look for an ashtray, then returned to the small-talk without having shed her involvement. He moved towards her under the same impulse that forced him invariably to answer a ringing telephone – he expected the news to be too tragic or too marvellous to be missed.

He thought: *To gain her attention he touched her lightly on the elbow.* It had started as a tic, involuntary but not really troublesome. During the last two days, though, it had become less easy to ignore – at times like a fierce itch in the brain. He tried to dismiss it as an errant form of selfconsciousness, but it was more persistent than that. He was giving himself stage directions. And although he acted without them most of the time, when the compulsion did nag at him it made him grind his teeth in rage. It was as if his life were towing him in its wake. He'd considered the ploy of proposing something impossible – *He flew to the moon* – but that didn't seem to wreck the process, which tolerated such tactics but pronounced them irrelevant.

To gain her attention he touched her lightly on the elbow. It must have been that she'd somehow spotted him crossing the room because without looking round she reached back and gripped his forearm, squeezing it, so as not to interrupt the man who was talking. Judging the conversation's peaks and troughs, she kept him on the edge of the circle for a little while longer, then drew him forward at the right moment to make introductions.

'Susan,' she said, 'and Paula and Deirdre and Rafe.'

They picked up the subject that had just been rested. The man said, 'No, it's perfectly simple: you tell us. In fact we usually ask the client, to be on the safe side. If you don't want your money invested in South Africa, say, or in an armaments company, or an outfit that tests lipstick by injecting rabbits with it, you say as much.' Rafe was wearing a careful, dark blue, three-piece suit with a red rosebud in the buttonhole; he looked perfectly at ease in this outfit. He'd swept the double-breasted jacket back at the sides in order to put his hands in his pockets, rather than use the vents. There was something to be read in this: it seemed to suggest that there were two ways of putting hands into pockets, one conventional and perfectly acceptable, the other rather dashing, a gesture which came naturally to only a few but which duller types, once they'd seen it, might remember to adopt.

Elaine arrived with more wine. 'Ah,' she said, 'you found one another.' She went from glass to glass, topping up, then stayed to talk to Paula and the circle broke up.

'What did you say that guy's name is?' he asked.

'Rafe.'

'Spell it.'

'R-a-l-p-h.'

'That's Ralph.'

'Some people pronounce it Rafe.'

'Why?'

'Don't start,' she said. 'Have you got any cigarettes?'

He handed her a packet. 'How do you know him?'

'University,' she said; then, before he could respond, 'You needn't get jumpy – just an acquaintance.'

'I gather he's a stockbroker.'

'Oh, God.' She drew on her cigarette and chuckled. As she exhaled she laughed louder, expelling the smoke in a series of swift gusts. 'He's harmless enough.'

'That's good.'

'Bit of a prick perhaps.'

'You think so, hey?'

Liking him came easily to her at times; for a reason she couldn't quite get to grips with, his petulance – its predictability – filled her with affection. At that moment she felt nothing could hurt them much, or threaten to divide them. They talked until the party drew them in.

An hour later he went into the kitchen to find another drink. It was empty apart from Susan and Deirdre who were passing a joint to and fro. Their mouths made tiny smacking noises, as if they were sucking their teeth. As he'd passed through the hallway, he'd thought: *He went into the kitchen to find another drink. He was very slightly tipsy and decided to make this glass of wine the last.* 'Shit,' he said, '*shit.*' Susan looked round the kitchen, frowning, trying to track down the object of his annoyance. She gave up and smiled in slow motion and offered him the joint. He took it, but handed it straight to Deirdre.

'It's good stuff,' Susan advised him; she sounded drowsy.

'Not tonight.' He found a cache of almost empty bottles that yielded a full glass. The party was thinning out, so his late arrival had been well timed. He drank the wine, barely remembering that the two women were there switching the joint back and forth; they sat at the table on wooden chairs, engrossed in the ritual. Their silence and the cautious motion of their hands borrowed something from the decorum of the waiting-room. With the last swallow of wine he felt his reserve slip a fraction. He was glad of it: maybe it would defeat this irksome business where actions were preceded by... And because the tiny loosening of composure struck him as a possible means to release, it also served as a reminder.

He thought: *He began to search among the bottles, looking for more dregs.* There might well have been something startling about the way he moved across the kitchen to the bottle-laden table: perhaps it was too quick, or began too suddenly; perhaps Susan and Deirdre were temporarily inhabiting a gentle, fragile, vegetarian world in which a calm smile took hours to spread and where speed and distress seemed raucous and demonic; whatever the reason, the two women shrank from his approach. He began to search among the bottles, looking for more dregs, although he hadn't at all wanted to; his hand went among the bottle necks, lifting and replacing. 'Shit,' he said. 'Shit, shit, *shit*.' A bottle went over, clattering among the rest, and as he grabbed for it his arm toppled two more. Others started to wobble. There was a short period when he had control of it – snatching and placing upright – then the domino effect got ahead of him and his rapid pursuit of the bottles became increasingly angry and frenetic until, outraged, he cuffed them this way and that, at the same time yelling, 'Bastard! You *bastard*!'

Susan was nearest. She shrieked, clambering over Deirdre to get away. She was crying, both hands in front of her mouth, and staring at him with a fixedness that came from the dope. She looked groggy and vulnerable. Glass snapped underfoot as she backed into some of the breakage. Like a child reacting to another's tears with tears of its own, Deirdre began to blub softly, looking at Susan as if to seek the reason. He put his hands on his hips, then dropped them to his sides again: an involuntary awkwardness that converted at once to irritation.

Elaine and Ralph entered the kitchen together and stood side by side. Their in-step appearance and sudden halt was somehow comic; having rushed in from the wings on cue, they now quivered on their chalk marks waiting for a prompt. Ralph moved first, going towards Susan, his arm already lifted to encircle her shoulders. 'What's this?' he asked. 'What the hell is going on?' – the sharp bark of an officer's voice.

'An accident,' he said. Elaine had fetched a dustpan and was crouching by his knees to collect the larger fragments. He stepped backwards to be out of the way, lifting his feet unnecessarily high. People drifted out of the drawing-room to congregate at the kitchen door. From the hallway she heard the rattle of glass as Elaine dropped the shards into the dustpan, and registered the tartness in Ralph's tone. She peered between heads, then pushed through into the kitchen.

'Are you all right?'

'Yes,' he said, without looking in her direction. 'Yes. Fine.'

Ralph lowered Susan into a chair, then moved centre-stage. 'Well – what happened?'

'Some bottles fell on the floor. It was an accident.'

'Is that all?' Ralph parted his jacket as before, sweeping each side back so that when he put his hands into his pockets the material was draped behind his wrists; then he looked sideways at the women, summoning the evidence of their damp faces. He flicked a glance at the jury assembled by the door. 'Why are they crying?'

'Ask them.'

'I'm asking you.'

Elaine passed between them with a full dustpan. He said, 'They're both stoned shitless – there's one clue. What's more, they possess many of the characteristics of the incurably stupid. Maybe that wraps up the case.' He turned his back. 'Come on, we're going.'

Ralph caught him by the shoulder, turning him and putting him slightly off-balance. 'No you're bloody not. We haven't finished yet.' There was a silence. A small horizontal crease had appeared on Ralph's upper lip together with a cluster of sweat-beads. He snickered. 'Come on – an explanation.'

He thought: *Grabbing Ralph's lapels, he pulled the man forward and butted him in the face* – jumping off his toes to lend impetus to the blow – then stepped back as Ralph hit the table and sat on it, covering his nose and mouth with one hand. Like most fights it was badly choreographed and inconclusive: bouts of ungainly action separated by ugly pauses. They wrestled and threw punches and knocked into things while a couple of men from the audience tried to separate them, darting in to pluck ineffectually at an arm or a piece of clothing. He took a hard clout under the eye; then Susan began to scream repeatedly, bending from the waist with each shriek like someone sneezing. Ralph flung out an arm and hit her backhanded across the face. 'Shut up, woman!' he yelled.

It was as if everyone in the room had exhaled at once. Elaine took Susan out of the room. People began to speak. Ralph made a loose gesture, hand out and palm uppermost, like a debater offering the floor to someone else. Blood from his nose had made a delta of rivulets over his mouth and chin and spotted the front of his collar. He turned away then, for some reason, took the rosebud out of his lapel and sniffed it.

She drove back smoothly enough, sitting well back from the wheel in her usual way, arms at full stretch, but kept letting go unnerving gouts of laughter – near hysterical cackles – and with each one gave him a wild-eyed glance. A swelling had started up on his cheekbone, narrowing his eye. If he looked through it, closing the other, the streets grew darker. A thin stalactite of pain had grown down to his jaw. He didn't resent her excitement but its odd, manic fervour wearied him. He made his seat recline so that his face was no longer in her line of vision. In an attempt to quieten her, he began to hum a tune and clasped his hands at the back of his neck. After a while it appeared to have an effect: her laughter diminished, then died, and she seemed to sit deeper in her seat. It was warm in the car. He gazed out, wanting the motion and the unbroken monotone of the engine to continue for a long time. Neat florets of sodium light traversed the windscreen.

They were home ten minutes later. The skin had broken over the swelling on his cheekbone and she put a chair alongside a lamp, making him sit there while she fetched some cotton-wool and a bottle of surgical spirit. She dabbed, then kissed him and dabbed again, her fingers under his chin to tilt his head. Her touch was unnecessarily light: maternal and flirtatious at the same time.

'Is Susan his wife?' he asked.

'His sister.'

It surprised him, and in some way led to a fleeting sympathy for Ralph: an affinity. She wiped a thread of blood from his cheek, then said: 'I met her once before. She was being shy and withdrawn, as I recall, though I remember thinking it was a bit of a pose. Three or four years ago. She's rather *solid*, isn't she? Sort of lumpy. And thick eyebrows. I always think that thick eyebrows probably go with heavy periods. Do you need a brandy or anything?'

'No,' he said; then, 'well, why not . . .'

She fetched them a drink apiece and sat on his lap while they sipped. He raised his heels and bounced her a few times. She giggled and began to talk about what had happened, her voice mellifluous with delight. Perhaps he ought to drop Elaine a note. No: on second thoughts she would do that; why should he have to offer apologies and so run the risk of appearing to admit culpability? Maybe Ralph had been drunk. Or could his aggression have stemmed from embarrassment at his bovine sister's outburst? Deirdre, she thought, shared a flat with Susan – a pair of druggy neurotics and well suited. Didn't she remember something about Susan having had a breakdown, or anorexia? . . . Well, not that, given her size, unless she'd gone to the other extreme and was now a compulsive eater. Ralph had been part of a dull set while at university – titled types with gels from the shires who visited them at weekends. They'd all had cars and were rather keen on japes. It sounded like a parody didn't it, but a few of that sort had still existed. Ralph's father, she thought, had been a captain of industry. Her tone put the term in inverted commas. She wondered whether his nose was broken. The embarrassment theory was most likely she decided: it provided the reason for Ralph having whacked his sister. How ridiculous they had looked – she with her lumpy, drugged face, wondering where the blow had come from, he with his junior-partner's suit and buttonhole, playing the role of inquisitor. No, she would write to Elaine – a jokey note but with a touch of indignation between the lines in order to fix the blame where it belonged.

Her earlier mood had given way to a form of lightheartedness. What *had* happened? she asked. He told her about the clutch of bottles falling: how it had started with one or two, but how next the circle of collapse had widened and become irretrievable, elaborating a little to make it funny. She laughed loudly, bouncing on his knees. It was a good story and he amused himself by telling it. She drank off her brandy and said, 'Let's go to bed.'

In the bathroom he swivelled his shaving-mirror to its magnifying side and examined the wound – a hard, almond-shaped welt dimpled by the cut and already showing some discoloration. His eye was bloodshot at the rim and throbbed irritatingly. He knew he would feel foolish, toting about this silly disfigurement. He would seem to himself to be like those people who display love-bites, or wear badges advertising their pacifism, or who stick decals on the rear windows of their cars to let others know that they attend classes in the martial arts. He always felt that such people were eager for comment, self-aggrandizing proselytizers for sex, peace, or discipline.

He thought: *He squeezed an inch of toothpaste on to the brush . . .* but it didn't go any further than that. When he reached the bedroom he found her asleep. The light was still on and she lay face-up, high on the pillows, with the bedcover barely drawn to her waist, as if sleep had surprised her as soon as she'd lowered her head.

*

It may have been that the fight in some way triggered the depression that, next day, began to afflict him; or not the fight so much as the peculiarities that attended it. He made an effort to think back, to try to identify his mood's origin, suspecting that if he were able to give it a name he would be able to control it. He could pinpoint nothing. Lethargy – always an early symptom – began to enfold him. Nothing as dramatic as a deadening of the will; just a cheerless indolence and lack of ideas. He felt mildly ill. The world started to fade at the edges, become monochromatic.

He experimented with remedies that had sometimes been effective. On a couple of days he drove to a pier on the embankment and took trips up and down the river, sitting out on deck to watch the rain twist and eddy across the smooth, opaque face of the Thames. Tourists jabbered, trooping from one rail to the other and wielding cameras fitted with gigantic lenses. The anonymity, and the knowledge that he was unreachable, pleased him and helped a little. He constructed playlets in which some life-altering thing had happened. The telephone rang and rang in an empty room; dramas developed while his absence grew more mysterious; troubled faces peered along hospital corridors; opportunities were missed.

For a day or two he was able to maintain a dismal *status quo*, then the depression closed in like bad weather in hill country. The temperature dropped and the light worsened. He walked complicated ten-mile circuits through the city's parks. He gambled: unlikely accumulator bets, or outsiders picked by an arcane association of ideas. He drank. Nothing made much difference. Strangely, the compulsion for depicting an action before he performed it helped to keep him mobile – each unbidden thought would provoke him to enact what he'd described. Between those times his dullness and bafflement increased.

He thought: *As the front door slammed, he paused as if he might change his mind, then walked down the steps and along the street to the car.* It would have been easy enough to call Elaine and tell her he was ill, but his sluggishness had prevented that. Too late now; but it didn't matter. His mood was such that choice had lost its potency. He was late, but the drive to Soho was free of hold-ups and he found a parking meter within yards of the restaurant. One of depression's eerier aspects – he'd noticed it before – was that it brought a sort of pointless luck. Small muddles and difficulties, because they had ceased to matter, formed neat patterns as he advanced on them.

There was a bookie's further along the road. He went in and put five pounds to win on a ten-to-one shot in a small race at Newbury, picking it solely for the odds, then backtracked to the restaurant. Elaine was reading a newspaper and affected to have not seen him until he reached the table. A Bloody Mary, untouched, stood alongside her still-folded napkin. She was smoking a pink cigarette. It occurred to him that she would be thought very attractive and wondered, briefly, what filled her life. They kissed cheeks and said hello, and she added, 'Sorry,' waving the cigarette. 'They come with the meal it seems.' On the table was a small sherry glass containing three more: turquoise, gold and black.

Their conversation switched this way and that, staying within predictable limits while at the same time looking beyond them, like a big-eyed fish in a tank. At times his mood reduced his voice to what seemed a humble murmur and she failed to hear him, but didn't ask for a repetition. When the meal was over, she lit the gold cigarette and said, 'It was very nice of you, but not at all necessary you know.'

'Well . . .' He shrugged. 'Perhaps not. I shouldn't have let things get out of hand.'

Elaine shook her head. 'Ralph was *looking* for it. I don't exactly know why.' She laughed. 'Found it, too.' As if she had only just noticed his quietness, his lack of appetite, the delicacy with which he touched objects on the table, she asked, 'Are you all right?'

'Oh, sure.' He put his fingertips to the swelling on his cheek which was puffier now, its inflammation fading to dull tones of olive and yellow.

'There was some family thing.' Elaine gestured vaguely with her cigarette, then stubbed it out rapidly. 'Some sort of – *undercurrent*, something going on between them all evening.'

He sensed that she was trying to intrigue him with this – was waiting to be drawn on the subject – so he said, 'Yes, I thought that must have been it.'

They fell silent for a few seconds, regarding one another uneasily, then Elaine made a little pout and laughed, just failing to pitch the sound at the right level for comfortable familiarity. 'Poor you,' she said. 'What a shiner.' And she covered his hand with her own, letting it lie a while before taking the turquoise cigarette. 'It's really unfair – I've done shamefully well out of a few broken bottles. Lunch from you, champagne from Ralph. I'm glad it was that way round.' She lit the cigarette and exhaled smoke to extinguish the match but also wagged her hand, then tweaked the cigarette from her lips – all action – as she said, 'The least I can do is offer you coffee and brandy *chez moi*.'

'That would be lovely,' he spread his arms to demonstrate regret. 'I'm meeting someone in fifteen minutes.'

As they parted, she delivered a tight, hard peck to his lips. He flagged down a taxi and handed her into it. 'Another time,' she stated, and he nodded as he slammed the door. Inside the cab she fussed with things in her handbag, not looking up as she gave the driver her address.

He watched her out of sight before walking down to the betting-shop. He tried to remember what she did for a living, then realized she must have taken the afternoon off. The thought unnerved him and he set it aside by counting the number of strides it took to get to the bookie's – twenty-five – then adding the digits – seven – which was a good omen because the horse had strolled in four lengths clear.

After that he wandered for an hour, quartering patches of the square mile and glancing all the time at the offers of peepshows

and stripshows and all-nude shows and shows that no one
should see who might be offended by the-sex-act-live-on-stage.
In the smaller streets, each doorway bore its ladder of cards:
Mona – Model – First floor. Carole – Model – First floor. Terri –
Model – First floor. He thought: *He pressed the bell and stepped
quickly into the dim hallway*. It was odd that the impulse had taken
so long to surface, and now that it had he said to himself, *Is that
all*? but there was no shadow-impulse to turn him back.

He was aware of passing someone on the stairs, of knocking
shoulders, then there was a door with Terri's card taped to it at
eye-level, then another door, then Terri who was pretty in a
sharp sort of way, and young. She was wearing a silk Chinese
jacket, unbuttoned, and nothing else. Her hair was blonde, cut
square at the shoulder, and it swung attractively as she came
towards him smiling like an old friend. He noticed that she had
a spider naevus on her left temple: a bleb of red tracery against
the whitest part of her skin.

He paid with his winnings. While he undressed she went to
a small paraffin heater by the bed-head and stood astride it,
cupping a hand between her legs and rubbing vigorously.
'Happiness is a warm pussy,' she said, ' – eh?' She crossed the
room and began to fondle him, peering curiously at his swollen
eye while her fingers were busy with his cock. Then she dropped
the jacket and said, 'Come on, darling.' They went to the bed
hand-in-hand. As he straddled her she reached down and
gripped him again. 'Oh,' she said, 'you're so *big*,' a piece of
professional flattery; but she spoke with her head turned away
and in what seemed a half abstracted manner – a reflexive *tut-
tut* – that sounded, for all the world, like the *sotto voce* aside of
a flummoxed housewife trying to find room, in an overcrowded
cupboard, for some redundant utensil.

She had called him 'darling' all the time. 'Forty pounds,
darling. That's right, darling. Unless you want something
special.'

'No,' he'd said, 'just . . . straight,' trying for a professional jargon himself. Then he had asked for something and she'd echoed his earlier thought: 'Is that all?' and smiled at his hesitancy. As he was leaving she'd said, 'See you again, darling,' and patted his bottom. He'd felt rather comforted by it.

The excursion had tired him. Driving home he scarcely thought about how the afternoon had passed. Defying the desire for inertia had been as taxing as walking into a gale. He strove for concentration, his hands slack on the steering-wheel, his feet ponderous. He couldn't imagine what it would be like to possess a swiftness and lightness of touch: to be brisk with the controls. After he'd parked the car he continued to sit in it for twenty minutes. *He got out of the car and locked it, then walked slowly towards* . . . Previously it had led him by the nose; now it offered an arm.

He sat in an easy chair and slept. When he woke the room was dark. A point of pain traversed his stomach like a radar blip, followed almost at once by another: the reason for his waking. At the back of his throat, clogged there, was a sour aftertaste of the fish he'd eaten at lunch. As the attack built, he went from room to room switching on the lights and looking about in the manner of one who hopes to find a misplaced cheque-book or a pair of glasses – some utilitarian aid. Within ten minutes it had become an agony. He sat on the lavatory yawning with disgust as the pain scored his abdomen like a steel stylus.

He emerged feeling brittle and feather-light, shivering so violently that he was made to stumble. The house was unnaturally silent and still, as it was when they came back to it after a holiday. Ordinary objects seemed to present evidence of the departure: a single glass on the draining-board, stale fruit in a bowl, a jacket hanging from the bedpost; the small oversights that make absence more marked. He went back to the armchair, taking a blanket with him. The chair was set in a corner of the room. He curled up beneath the blanket and looked round at the array of their possessions, his glance sharpening now and then like an auctioneer's. For some reason the attack had left him with a heightened sense of smell, uncomfortably acute, as though his nasal membrane had been scoured. There came a waft of heavy perfume – not Terri's; some residue from another room. Then there was a more constant, fragile, tang of iodine – an inexplicable memory of the sea – and, hanging beneath that, the rich, nutty scent of his ordure. He detected in it the taint of his own extinction. It was an old man's smell.

By the time she arrived home he had developed a slight fever. The illness constrained him – a comfortable sensation. The fever's heat and the blanket swaddled him; and there was nothing he had to do but wait it out. She could sense his withdrawal. She put down her briefcase and a bag of shopping and drew the curtains, then went to stand beside him, testing his forehead and cheeks with the back of her hand.

'What is it?' she asked. Then – amused – 'You look like a squaw.'

'I don't know. Food poisoning I think.' He suffered her to smooth his hair. 'My eyeballs feel dusty.'

'Do they?' She smiled and stooped to kiss the top of his head. 'You'd better go to bed. Is there anything you want?'

'No,' he said, 'I'm okay here. Chat to me. Don't go away.'

She knew he enjoyed the role and was content to indulge him. Paradoxically, his self-absorption demanded a companion, a nurse, an observer; anyone would have done as well. She took the shopping into the kitchen and made herself a cup of tea, then returned to him. He was watching the door, bright-eyed.

'Did you see Elaine for lunch?'

He nodded. 'Sends her love.'

'And that's where you ate whatever . . .'

'Must have been.'

'Will she have got it too?'

'Don't think so. She had veal; I had fish.' He shivered.

'Ah –' She raised her eyebrows. 'Fish.'

They discussed the shortcomings of restaurateurs. He repeated what Elaine had told him: 'Some family thing –' They talked about Elaine for a time – her failed marriage, her job – then about a country they'd been planning to visit. At one point she filled a hot-water bottle and lifted the blanket to place it against his stomach. She mentioned a phone call from a friend inviting them to dinner the following week and read aloud, from that day's paper, a review of a film they'd agreed they wanted to see. She sat close to him, on the very arm of his chair, or moved weightlessly among the objects in the room seeming, all the time, to grow quieter and more remote. He could feel the depression lifting minute by minute.

THE FIFTH YEAR

*

29 September–5 October

She had just entered the hall, carrying a large store-bag in either hand. A bunch of flowers was trapped under one arm; the other was held almost horizontally to prevent her shoulder-bag from dragging along the floor: it had slipped down and was caught by its strap across her wrist. That had probably happened when she'd put her house keys back (using the less burdened hand) a moment before nudging the door with her hip to open it fully. The effect was to make it seem that she was holding the store-bag up for inspection: you could read the designer's name, and 'Knightsbridge' underneath. She was standing on her right foot, the left extended backwards to hook the door, to slam it, and had on her face the look of blind concentration people wear when feeling for something out of sight. Very shortly she'd find it. The door would close and she would become animate again, putting down the bags with a *woof* of relief, laying the flowers on the hall table and then, perhaps, removing her beret in order to shake out her hair. The rain had been heavy and there was a strong wind. When she'd raised her foot that way, a gust had got into the skirt of her topcoat and belled it like a crinoline.

The beret was a piece of good luck. She'd been wearing it when they'd first met. Since then, of course, her hairstyle had changed many times; it was short now, but he remembered that she had once worn the beret sloping away from her crown like a schoolgirl, her hair fanning out beneath it and on to her shoulders. Her face had been a little flushed, her eyes bright, and she'd been slightly breathless but, nonetheless, full of swift action. She had peeled the beret off backwards to avoid disarranging her hair and then crossed the room to greet her hostess. There had been delight and energy in her laugh. Years later he'd reminded her of the scene and asked whether she had come from a lover. She'd replied that, yes, she had been with someone that morning but walking, just walking, circumnavigating the Round Pond again and again while she tried to decide how best to finish matters. It had been a lunch party. She'd been the last to arrive because of the time it had taken to break out of the circle and find a cab in the Bayswater Road.

On her lapel was a brooch he'd given her that she scarcely ever wore. He would see when she took off the topcoat that the rest of her outfit was new; the skirt, sweater and boots she'd been wearing were in the store-bags. He couldn't have said why she almost always came home with flowers after buying new clothes.

Now she was looking into the mirror that hung above the bathroom sink. She was naked and stood with her weight on one leg, so that her hip on that side was slightly hoisted, and she leaned forward like someone about to peer round a corner: a posture that brought her right eye towards the glass. A cotton swab, doused in make-up remover, was halfway to her face. Her body was uneven: a straight leg, and the buttock clenched on the side farther from where he stood; then, almost within touching distance, one arm lifted, lifting the breast a little, too, and the eye closing as she prepared to wipe it. Her belly was just convex, but taut – almost muscular. Because the swab was approaching, her mouth had gone slack and it was possible to see a glisten of saliva on the fullest part of her lower lip.

After the cleansing she would have sprayed her face and neck with water from an atomizer, tilting her head back and arching her spine so that it sank to a deep fosse from shoulderblades to waist; then brushed her hair; then attended to her clothes, folding some neatly and restoring them to drawers and cupboards, separating others to be washed. When her spine did that he wanted to fillet her. He had watched her preparations so many times that he'd memorized the order of things. Had she varied it, or skipped a stage, he might have protested as a child will if a bored parent should start to condense a bedtime story.

They had decided to go through their books and take those they no longer wanted to a charity shop. It was impossible, she'd said, to accommodate one more book. The shelves were solid; every flat surface in the place had its pile of books. After two hours the rejects numbered seven: a pointlessly small pile on the dining-room table. They had spent most of the time browsing and now she sat with an open book propped against the condemned few and read while she ate some soup and a salad sandwich.

The book was *Pilgrim's Progress*, though you couldn't see that. It was, he thought, the kind of thing you read only when you were having a clear-out. Although her eyes were on the page, she'd ducked her head to bite into the sandwich and had turned it a little to the left as she tugged at the crust: there was a small bulge of tension in her jaw that would be visible to anyone who knew the planes of her face. A creamy runnel of mayonnaise was trickling across her palm and it was evident that she knew it was there, since her left hand – cupped – was above the table, positioned to catch the drip if it fell before she'd bitten off her mouthful. She looked awkward but unhurried. He liked the fact that her concentration seemed largely unbroken – the cupped hand a near-unthinking response to the tiny, impending accident. Much of her face was invisible.

Oddly, he couldn't remember which of them owned *Pilgrim's Progress*. There had been very little duplication of either books or records. He thought, on reflection, that it must be his and wondered how he'd come by it.

'We're so alike, you know,' she'd said to him once. 'I have this nightmarish vision of the two of us in old age becoming like those gentle, geriatric twosomes who endlessly anticipate one another: clichés of elementary ESP. I'll think, "Time the roses were pruned", and a little later you'll shuffle off in your carpet slippers and gardening gloves to get the secateurs from the tool-shed; or I'll put a cup of tea on the table, close to where you're working, and you'll look up and say, "Oh, I was just thinking . . ." ' She had shivered. 'We'll sort of *merge*.'

He'd laughed and said, 'Very unlikely; in any event, I can't help feeling that you ought to have nobler fears.'

She'd persisted. 'We'll have little routines to cocoon us. By then, we'll know how to avoid the things we hate doing and things we like will be apportioned in weekly rations.'

'And between times?'

'Anticipation without excitement.'

'Shared anticipation?'

'Yes.'

'No surprises?'

'Worse – no secrets.'

'Aha,' he'd said, 'yes, I see.'

The seven books were all holiday reading: some whodunnits, a few writers recommended by friends. Judging by its direction, the mayonnaise would reach her wrist-bone before dripping into her waiting hand, unless she first licked it off.

Now she was in the bath and everything about her was inelegant. One foot was drawn up and lodged on the bath's sill; she was leaning forward, grasping the foot with her left hand and wielding nail clippers with the right. Hunched over that way she distorted her likeness. Her breasts became thin and conical; two parallel bulges, not large, but noticeable, ran across her abdomen; her upper arms appeared disproportionately thick; her pubic hair looked a tangle. She regarded him across her raised knee, her features exaggerated and made hard by the mob-cap that covered her hair. It was unjust; her figure was close to perfect and her features, although they possessed few classic lines, were always striking, sometimes beautiful. She looked neither surprised nor resentful. Rather, she wore the expression of one who expects she is about to receive some mildly disappointing news: resigned, wry, but largely unconcerned. The manner in which she presented herself to the world was not a matter of careful construction but of flair. It struck him that to observe her at that moment – with the lines of her body askew – was to see something untypical, and the thought pleased him.

Now she was preparing food and, for a moment, had stopped at the sink. Whatever task she had just performed had made her want to wash her hands. Along the length of the work-surface was an assortment of bowls and pots and ingredients. A skillet had been placed over a gas-jet and she was glancing over her shoulder to check on the progress of whatever was cooking in it, while her hands remained under the flow of water. She looked competent and preoccupied. She'd had to lean back for a clear view, so her arms were at full stretch; her hands were folding round the soap; her face was turned. But for the expression of calm capability, her pose would have resembled that of a heroine from some Victorian melodrama pleading with a stony-hearted landlord. Her profile was just as he'd hoped to see it.

Now she was looking directly at him and laughing. Her evening dress was so scant and so well cut that its thin straps seemed to bear no weight but lay lightly across her collarbones. She stood beside a lamp – had been about to switch it off – and its light gave her hair, on that side, the faintest patina of red. In her raised hand she held a small satin clutch-bag containing lipstick, a mirror, a comb. Her necklace, a chain of gold scallops, dipped into the hollow at her throat. On the wall behind her head was a small watercolour he'd given her two years before and which they'd both come to dislike: a purplish cloud filling the sky above a plain of corn, or over a beach perhaps; its openness to interpretation aroused contempt in him.

She lobbed the bag and he caught it, one-handed, just in front of his face. 'How long is this going to continue?' she asked, still laughing. 'Every time I stop moving I hear the click of a shutter-release.' He shrugged, ignoring the plain invitation to join her laughter: to make a game of it. Instead, he returned the bag, set the camera down on a nearby table and led her to the front door.

They found a taxi easily and he settled into the seat, leaving it to her to give their destination. After a short silence, he asked, 'You don't mind – that it's Bohème?'

'Don't be silly. It's your birthday. It's nice of you to share your present.'

'You bought the tickets.'

'I know, but one of them's for me after all.' She looked fondly at him. 'I imagine you'll weep discreetly during the first duet: as usual.'

'No doubt. Evidence of my limitless capacity for being moved by cheap sentiment. As a child I could always be counted on to lead the clapping that would keep Tinkerbell alive – clapped till my little hands were numb and howled like a fucking siren. A lot of experts despise the opera, you know. Think it trite. Even Puccini admitted to having more heart than head.'

'A grievous flaw,' she said, 'as we know. I'll make your Christmas present a trip to *Peter Pan*.'

'No. What I'd like for Christmas is a scapegoat.'

'I'll try Harrods.'

'I was thinking of getting away for a bit, on my own,' he said.

'Were you?'

'Just for a bit.'

She kept quiet. It might have been that she was giving the idea some thought. In the taxi, in the half-light, on the way to a crowded auditorium and the distraction of the music, his boldness seemed – to him at least – unportentous.

She said, 'Sure. Of course. If you want to.'

'Just for a while.' A thread of pain ran into his lap and he transformed his wince into a smile.

'Yes,' she said, 'of course.'

Now she was posing coquettishly. Halfway across the bedroom, approaching the bed, she'd paused when he'd raised the camera and was standing with her right arm bent at the elbow and partially covering her breasts, her left hand extended to rest lightly on her bush. Her lips were pursed in mock-outrage, a little, prim 'O' – as cleverly done as the tilt of her head and the seductive sideways glance. She had been about to hang her evening dress in the wardrobe and had dropped it to take the pose: a crumple of silk that lay about her ankles like an erotic prop.

Now she was pulling on her jeans, bending forward to tug at the waistband which, in that instant, was at the tops of her thighs. Her back was towards the camera – she'd been peering out of the window to check on the weather – but she must have heard some give-away sound because she was looking at him over her shoulder, favouring him with a broad, lecherous wink and thrusting her bottom backwards like a showgirl. A little to the left, on a chest of drawers, was a photograph of himself standing by a Scottish loch and next to that the jumble of jewellery she'd worn on the previous evening.

Now she was reading a newspaper: or, rather, looking over it in response to having heard him call her name. Something had faltered in her smile. She wore the slightly embarrassed and apprehensive look of one who has misinterpreted a remark or gesture and made some inappropriate response. Above her chair was a mirror which had reflected the stab of light from the flashgun, though his presence was occluded by the glare.

Now she was using the phone, her mouth awkward with whatever she was pronouncing, but her eyes were on him filled with puzzlement and annoyance. You could see how her concentration was slipping, how she was stranded between the fact of his sudden attention to her and the voice on the line. She was seated, her head and torso inclined away from him – the sort of avoiding action someone will take to get out of a bee's flightpath; and although the phone was to her ear and she apparently in mid-sentence, it would be impossible to agree, simply by looking at the photograph, that she was still talking to the anonymous caller.

Now she was getting up from the lavatory seat, a wad of yellow tissue in her left hand, her right flung out in the direction of the lens, fingers spread. It was evident that he had anticipated her movement to block him, because he'd sidestepped to get the shot.

Her defence in all this lacked deftness. She recognized the skill with which he had, at first, recruited both her vanity and her tendency to be amused by eccentricity; but by the time she had realized that there was something less than spontaneous going on, she had lost track of any clues that might have helped her to identify its source.

About a week, and pretty much non-stop . . . Arriving home, going out, bedtimes, mornings, eating, ironing, a whole sequence while she slept (she'd grown furious for being woken, each time, by the flash), bathing, cooking – taking a piss, for Christ's sake! There was something both sullen and smug about the way he would appear, all in a rush, unspeaking, squinting and clicking and winding on – something farcical, too, and threatening, but she now accepted that that was part of the exercise. She'd said, 'It's stopped being funny, you know. What's it all for?' and he'd shrugged, then tapped the side of his nose as if to say, 'Don't ask. Does it matter? Wait and see . . . a surprise, perhaps.' It might be best, she decided, to let him tire.

It was their fifth year together and she still couldn't devise any method for their day-to-day living. The placidity of companionship, the pleasant mindlessness of routine, the ease that inattention brings – everything she'd once thought of as likely to deaden a marriage – seemed rare and unattainable. Too often, their love resembled something forced and gaudy – out of season. Taking the tube to work that morning, she had stared at her portrait in the window opposite as the train rocked and banged through the tunnel and wondered whether marriage might be the answer.

The restaurant was crowded with people eating expense-account lunches, but that wasn't evident. You could see only two tables apart from hers. At one of them a waiter was bending from the waist and manipulating vegetables on to a plate, using a fork and spoon which were gripped, dextrously, in one hand. She had given up on her almost untouched food and was holding a water glass, though she appeared not to be about to drink from it. The point of her elbow was on the table; her fingers nipped the glass by its rim, suspending it six inches or so above the table-top. Her free hand was slightly in advance of the glass, palm upwards and tilted slightly to emphasize a point. She looked knowledgeable and committed.

He had always known that she inhabited her life outside with an eagerness born of ambition and unalloyed pleasure. Her professional talent was intuitive; she used it as a water-diviner uses his rod; it was unobtrusive and negotiable, like currency. All of this, he thought, lay in her gesture, her corrupt half-smile. A lock of hair which had strayed across her cheek was disarming to just the right degree.

In the second shot, the waiter had straightened up. He was looking at the camera and grinning, though it was clear that, in a second, he would turn his attention to the subject of the photograph – a celebrity, surely? Her companion – a woman – had swivelled in her chair, attracted by the flash-gun, and was smiling too, but hers was a smile of incomprehension: the expression you'll see on the face of someone who has just been warmly greeted by a complete stranger.

The glass was still suspended but tilted now, and the upturned palm withdrawn. Her eyes were almost closed, only a sliver of white showing above the lower lid, and from the angle of her torso it appeared that she might be about to rise. It looked like a botched holiday snap: 'Oh dear, this isn't very good. You probably weren't ready.' He noticed that her briefcase, which had been standing alongside her chair, had toppled over. What you didn't get from the photograph was the sudden silence.

That night he lodged himself against the jamb of the bedroom door like a hesitant visitor to a sickroom. She lowered her book and pushed it a little to one side: a gesture designed to make him aware that she would pick it up again in a moment. She made hardly any shape at all under the crisp bedclothes.

They were both exhausted. He had spent the evening stone-walling. 'I was passing. I know you always eat there. It was just a daft impulse. Christ, where's your sense of humour?' She'd been sickened by the way he struggled to sound plausible. He'd drunk whisky and chortled dismissively, offering to write a note of apology to her lunch-date, his tone of voice implying that nothing could be less necessary. She had stalked from room to room in search of the camera, but when she found it and opened the back it was empty of film.

She watched him standing half in, half out of the room and listened to what he'd rehearsed, which was no more than an elaborate, less believable, version of what he'd said before, then teased the book back into her grasp. 'Please.' He stumbled out for another drink and sat with it for a while. When he returned the light was out. He switched it on at the door and she reared up in the bed and screamed. As he began to speak, began to advance, she fought past him and took a pill from a phial on the dressing-table. When she tried to pass again, he stopped her by catching her at the throat with his free hand. Whisky slopped on to the carpet. She stood completely still, head canted backwards, while he held her. When his hand dropped she crossed to the bed, got in, turned out the light and lay still.

He took the whisky bottle with him and went outside and sat in the car. He drank a couple of mouthfuls from the bottle, then started the engine and drove three or four streets away before turning back and parking by the iron gates of a municipal park in sight of the house. He'd left the drawing-room lights burning and the curtains drawn back. The room looked like a stage set: as if, at any moment, actors would appear from the wings and take their positions before delivering crucially informative opening lines.

He dozed, then woke as the bottle fell from between his thighs. A dog was whining nearby, the only sound in the street. Looking sideways, he saw it standing on the other side of the padlocked gate, its snout through the bars. Its white coat was tinted pink by the sodium lights. When he got out of the car it backed off, still whining, expecting to be let out. He wandered a few yards to both left and right looking for a gap in the wire fencing, but it was secure. The dog followed him to and fro until they came back to the gate. He rattled the padlock and chain, moving the gate slightly, and the dog put its fore-paws on the concrete gate-post. Then it turned and ran off into the shrubbery.

He went back to the car and slept. The grind and rumble of a refuse lorry woke him. Dustmen were yelling, emerging from basements with bins hefted on their shoulders. A radio was playing in the cab; the driver leaned out and bawled jokes at his workmates as he inched the vehicle along the street.

The drawing-room lights were still on. He switched them off and pulled the curtains to before undressing. The bedroom was a bowl of pale light. She had kept to her side of the bed and seemed not to have moved at all or disturbed the neatness of the bedclothes. He eased himself in beside her, getting as close as possible to the fusty warmth, and went to sleep immediately.

It was after ten-thirty when he woke again and the place was empty. A tap was dribbling in the bathroom sink; the bath was damp and there were a few springy hairs near the plughole. He lathered his face and began to shave. After he'd taken the foam off his neck and made the stroke from just under one ear to the point of the jaw, he stopped and sat on the edge of the bath to smoke a cigarette. Then he went back into the drawing-room and finished the glass of whisky he'd abandoned the night before.

*

Now she was one of many – a swell of people emerging from an underground station and crowding the pavement. Her face was towards him – she hadn't yet taken her direction for home – but he was on the other side of the road, invisible for being unexpected. A draught from the tunnel had gushed up to meet a breeze in the street and the vortex had snatched one side of her scarf so that it fluttered stiffly before her, like a pennant. The arrested motion of those around her underlined their urgency. To her right, two teenagers were embracing and the other travellers were parting to go around them. The boy wore mittens and his hands looked lumpish on the girl's back. To her left, and just ahead, a man was raising the collar of his overcoat. Fixed in the moment, he stood with his elbows jutting on either side of his head, looking for all the world as if he were tugging madly at his ears.

Alone among strangers, she possessed a certain poise; not so much aloofness as no sense of lack. Much later, he would look at the photograph and puzzle over this. It was something akin to grace, but not merely that . . . the patience and calm assuredness of a gambler riding his luck.

After she had turned and begun to walk away he'd snapped her again. She was becoming anonymous, her head and upper back boxed-in by others and blurred by lights and distance; although if it were your purpose, you could still have picked her out by the fact that she was taller than most of the women and many of the men. Not more than a minute later she would take a sidestreet to the right, allowing him a glimpse of her face – a pale smudge, at that distance, in contrast to the dark material of her coat. By the time he focussed she'd be gone; and, in trying to preserve it, he would miss the moment of her going.

THE FIFTH YEAR

*

16 October –

The rainstorm had lasted five or six minutes. Purple clouds bunched like deformities beneath the thin grey film that had blocked the sun all morning and then the small town was hosed over in a sudden frenzy of downpour. Between the close rows of houses in the backstreets the light was a livid gleam on wet stone.

He had retreated from the first fat drops, able to tell from the eclipse-like darkness what was coming. He'd gone back into the restaurant bar and asked for another cognac, then had angled his bar stool so that he could watch the rain funnelling down the steep hill directly towards him, sluicing the striped awnings and the *quincaillerie*'s display of hardware. The plaster horse's head outside the *boucherie-chevaline* had glistened and seemed bowed as if it were hauling a load against the slope. He'd watched over the shoulders of the two young men playing the pinball machine, until the rumble of the downpour had given way to a lighter note of water emptying into gratings and there had been nothing more than a thin tangle of silver in the wind; then he'd put on his cap, zipped his jacket, and walked through the empty streets to the church.

The pavements were awash. His feet were soaked by the time he got there. As the green baize door thumped to behind him, there was a scuffling nearby. Three children were grouped behind the nearest pew looking up at him like animals about to be put to flight, one with his hand still on the open flap of the poor-box, the other two with fists clenched and held straight down as if they were carrying laden buckets. They watched to see whether he would approach them or speak; then, a tiny herd, they feinted towards the far door, checked, bunched, and ran.

He took a three-franc candle and walked to where the statues of the saints stood in their niches, hesitating a moment before clipping it into one of the spring-grips in front of St Teresa. The flame drew out as the thin tip of wax burned off. The pain hit him and held, so that he had to bend forward, the heel of his hand pressed into his lap. Finally it drained away. He sat down and met the placid stare of the saint.

His prayer was a random, repetitive, inexpert thing. He prayed like a child: backtracking to apologize, fumbling, pausing, trying to hold certain thoughts at bay, stammering through the preposterous, ripe vocabulary. He gave up quite soon and simply repeated a single plea: take it away; please take it away.

From beneath his closed eyes there stepped the image of Terri. She crossed the room to stand astride the heater and rubbed herself, cupping her hand over that corruption as if to avoid spilling any. She called him 'darling'. She walked towards him, her square-cut blonde hair swinging, and he saw, between her hips, a hive swarming with putrefaction in each cell: honey and poison.

By the time he had driven fifty miles south, the sky had cleared. The sun was low: an intense red light flickering on and off like a strobe-lamp when he passed through the long avenues of plane trees that seemed to be on the outskirts of every small town. He drove badly: too fast and with little attention. The hired Renault 4 wallowed on bends and the steering-wheel oscillated violently when he pushed the car over eighty. He sat and drove, barely noticing the car's performance.

Before dark he pulled in to a filling station and used a little of his barbaric French. 'Essence super. À plein.' He got out of the car, leaving the woman attendant to fill the tank, and walked round the side of the white concrete building to the lavatory. For a moment, as he stood in front of the tiled trough, his mind went blank: the vacuity of the first second or two of voiding. Then a pain took him. He jerked forward, making an errant movement with his hand, and his head cracked against the metal frame of the open window. A jet of piss splashed his left trouser leg. After he'd recovered he could feel a trickle of blood gathering along his eyebrow. There was no mirror in the room, so he dabbed at the wetness with his sleeve, then went back to the forecourt. The woman was screwing the cap back on to his petrol tank. She stared at his face as he handed her a hundred-franc note; he knew she was looking at the blood. After another sixty miles he stopped and took a drink from his flask.

He looked in the driving mirror and picked off some of the dried flakes of blood with a fingernail. It was ten o'clock and still light. He'd stopped the car in a pebble-strewn lay-by just in sight of the next village, intending to spend the night sleeping on the back seat. After smoking three cigarettes one after the other, he put a Mogadon on his tongue and washed it down with a gulp of brandy from the flask.

When he woke it was just dawn. The road was empty. The ditches by the roadside were awash with mauve shadow. He got out of the car and stretched, wincing as the pain came but able to ignore it. A second, stronger pain made him stumble against the driver's door and he paused, head bowed, waiting for it to pass. Then he got in and completed the drive to Toulouse.

He parked the car near the centre and found a shop where he could buy a map. Les Jacobins was shown, but he couldn't tell how far he'd have to walk. The sun was hot now and the city becoming crowded. He walked from street to street, checking his position on the map from time to time, noticing almost nothing of his surroundings: just the names of the streets. After forty minutes he stopped and sat down on the corner of a broad set of steps that led to a municipal building. He felt intensely lonely. For a moment he panicked, desperate at being stranded in a strange city, alone, barely remembering how he'd got there, scarcely able to speak the language. He felt sick and unpleasantly lightheaded and deeply unhappy. The pavements had a curious pungency, as if there had been rain. He sat for a while with his

palms over his face, breathing shallowly, trying to picture her.
He could get bits and pieces, but the face wouldn't cohere. It
seemed likely that she would be following her routine: filling
her day responsibly, contributing to meetings, taking phone
calls, responding to questions; perhaps she'd have one or two
dinner engagements with visiting businessmen. He saw her
smiling and chatting brightly, or standing bare-breasted before
her wardrobe deciding what to wear.

He felt lost. He felt he should be running the streets, searching
for something familiar. He wanted to be back. Five minutes or
so passed before he got up and crossed the street to a small
pâtisserie where he bought a plastic bottle of mineral water and
half-a-dozen small yellow cakes. He ate two of the cakes as he
walked, saturating each mouthful with a swallow from the
bottle.

Almost by accident, he found Les Jacobins. It had seemed
there would be further to go, but the scale of the map had
deceived him. The place seemed like a barn. He stood twenty
paces in from the door and looked up at the palm-tree pillars,
then across to the tomb in the centre of the floor. A woman was
kneeling before it, praying; others, behind her, were waiting
their turn. He too would have to wait. The pain nagged at him
so that he shook his head and thumped his knuckles against his
thigh. He went outside and sat on the low brick wall, sweating
into his clothes.

The sun had given him a mild headache. Someone sitting
next to him on the wall spoke, then nudged him gently on the
arm: a boy of about eleven or twelve; he was saying something
about money. The pain came and he clutched at his groin
involuntarily, bending forward, knocking the paper bag with
the cakes in it on to the paving stones. The boy watched him,
laughing loudly; then he hopped off the wall and retrieved the
bag. As he handed it back he mentioned money again and his
face grew serious.

He didn't move, so the boy leaned forward and patted him,
touching his fly. He understood almost nothing that was being

said, but he thought he guessed what the boy was offering. Picking up the cakes and the water, he went back into the church, knowing he was being followed, and bought two tickets for the cloisters. The boy was close behind, half grinning like someone waiting to be introduced.

A few students, books open before them, were occupying the sunny triangle of grass at the near end of the cloisters. He walked to the apex of the section in shade and waited for the boy to catch up. To his right was a gloomy little chapel, its flagstones covered in dust. A few wooden chairs were set out before the altar; much of the rest of the space inside was taken up by pieces of broken masonry. A candle was burning on one shelf of the altar before a small, bruised statuette. He pointed to a chair, then sat beside the boy and bent over in prayer. 'Let it be taken from me . . .' He didn't know how to improve on the silly, archaic language. 'Let it be taken away . . .'

He opened the bag and gave the boy a cake, then took the plastic cap from the bottle and handed that over too. The boy bit off half a cake and took a sip of water, drooling it slightly; he looked puzzled for a second, then he laughed again and some of the soggy cake, the sin, spilled on to his chin as he tried to speak through the mouthful. The drivel of baby-talk, ill-formed, the vacuous look in the blue eyes, conveyed nothing. He took the boy's hand and pushed the remnant of cake towards his open, laughing mouth. The hand resisted; then the boy jumped off the chair, still laughing, and ran towards the broken pillars by the wall, ducking behind the first, emerging further down the line, then disappearing again in order to pop up and peer round a soot-covered slab near the door.

The boy giggled as he was caught and led back to his chair but he wouldn't take another cake or hold the water bottle. 'Eat it. You must eat.' He held a cake against the soft lips, trying to concentrate on keeping the prayer going. The boy struggled, turning his head and tugging against the grip on his arm. Without giving thought to the action he drew back his free arm and slapped the boy across the side of the face. Then he proffered

181

the water and cakes again. The boy ate, forcing the food, gagging and letting wet nuggets of cake fall from his mouth. Another slap banged his head sideways. He took the cake that was being held out to him and pushed it into his mouth. The bottle neck grazed him as it was thrust against his teeth, tilted, and held there. He cried, a thick runnel of snot glistening on his lips. There was a sharp pain where his hair was being gripped. He choked against the sog of cake and water, opening his mouth for air, then began to gag horribly, able neither to swallow nor breathe. His face went a deep red. He felt the hands release him and he fell forward, gargling the mush in his throat, then ran from the chapel, his arms wagging, awkward, at his neck.

He waited for fifteen minutes after the boy had gone, but no one came. The spilled water had made a black puddle on the flagstone under the boy's chair. A mess of broken cake lay in it.

Out in the street he tried to retrace his steps to the car, got lost, and eventually came to a road close by the river. He went down stone stairs to the strip of riverside grass and trudged half a mile before resting on a bench. The pain came and went. Power-boats and boats ferrying tourists passed every few minutes.

He sat through the afternoon, and sat on as dusk began to blot out the buildings on the far bank. The grass darkened and became trackless. Streetlamps came on and lamps in houseboats at the water's edge. From time to time, less often now, some vessel passed. Marooned there, he watched the points of light scamper and stretch in the backwash.

MORE ABOUT PENGUINS, PELICANS, PEREGRINES AND PUFFINS

For further information about books available from Penguins please write to Dept EP, Penguin Books Ltd, Harmondsworth, Middlesex UB7 0DA.

In the U.S.A.: For a complete list of books available from Penguins in the United States write to Dept DG, Penguin Books, 299 Murray Hill Parkway, East Rutherford, New Jersey 07073.

In Canada: For a complete list of books available from Penguins in Canada write to Penguin Books Canada Ltd, 2801 John Street, Markham, Ontario L3R 1B4.

In Australia: For a complete list of books available from Penguins in Australia write to the Marketing Department, Penguin Books Australia Ltd, P.O. Box 257, Ringwood, Victoria 3134.

In New Zealand: For a complete list of books available from Penguins in New Zealand write to the Marketing Department, Penguin Books (N.Z.) Ltd, Private Bag, Takapuna, Auckland 9.

In India: For a complete list of books available from Penguins in India write to Penguin Overseas Ltd, 706 Eros Apartments, 56 Nehru Place, New Delhi 110019.